"How'd you guys like to go on a stickup with me?"

## LISTEN TO JOE. HE HAS IT
## ALL FIGURED OUT.

"I said, how's about we all go on a stickup? It's foolproof. If it works, we'll be in great shape. If not, maybe they'll give us three years . . . maybe . . . and that would be free room and board and when we'd get out we'd each have thirty-six Social Security checks waiting for us. And that, by the way, adds up to eight thousand, five hundred and thirty-two bucks . . . apiece. Not a bad hunk of change. Maybe we could all put it together and buy one of them newspaper and candy stands in one of them big buildings in Manhattan. A friend of mine's son bought him one and he lives pretty good. But what the hell am I talking about that for? That's only if we get caught . . . and I don't think we'd get caught."

**IT'S THE PERFECT CRIME . . . almost.**

## GOING IN STYLE

# GOING IN STYLE

### A Novel By
## ROBERT GROSSBACH

### From The Screenplay By
## MARTIN BREST

### Based On A Short Story By
## EDWARD CANNON

**WARNER BOOKS**

A Warner Communications Company

WARNER BOOKS EDITION

Copyright © 1979 by Warner Books, Inc.
All rights reserved.

ISBN: 0-446-92485-7

Warner Books, Inc., 75 Rockefeller Plaza, New York, N.Y. 10019

Ⓦ A Warner Communications Company

Printed in the United States of America

First Printing: December, 1979

10 9 8 7 6 5 4 3 2 1

# Prologue

It had been four years since Joe had last eaten dogfood. Cycle Four had been advertised as especially suited for "the older pooch, the dog who may have difficulty chewing, who may not get around like he used to." That's me, Joe had thought sardonically. The older pooch.

He hadn't liked it. "I'll take Alpo or Carnation any time over that crud," he'd said, and Willie and Al had laughed, although it wasn't funny. Joe had been a braggart. "I was eatin' dogfood before it became popular," he'd crowed. He was the most adventuresome of the three old men, or the most foolhardy, depending on one's point of view. It was Joe who had proposed they all move into one apartment. "Share the misery," was his phrase.

"I don't think I can get along with anybody,"

7

said Willie, and he went on to explain that thirty-nine years of driving a cab had soured him on humanity. "Not that you guys aren't the best, dearest friends a man could have," he added, "but, still, *living* with you . . ." He lowered his head and, with a peculiar, horse-like motion, shook it from side to side.

Al was not too hot on the idea either. "Never did room with anyone," he explained. "Man or woman."

"How about beast?" asked Joe.

"That neither," said Al, "although I did have some plants. I like my privacy, you know. That's why I'd never go into one of them nursin' homes."

Joe had rolled his eyes skyward. "So you'd rather stay where you are, is that it? Keep the status quo. Tell yourselves that two hundred fourteen dollars a month is really providin' ya with 'social security.' You feel secure, walkin' down the streets of Corona? You feel secure lyin' in bed with a fever, not able to afford a bottle aspirin? You feel secure wearin' the same trousers for two weeks in a row, because you can't take your other pair out of the cleaners till your check comes? Does it give you a good rush to see some mutt on TV diggin' his snoot into the same thing you just ate for dinner?"

Willie and Al remained silent.

"Ah, but our sensitive personalities *might* not harmonize in one large apartment," continued Joe, "so we better let it go. Preferable to continue on like we are." He shrugged. "Oh well, it was just a thought."

Of course, it was only a matter of time before he had reasoned and shamed them into it. Joe was a master at that, Mr. Hard Guy and Mr. Softy rolled

8

into one aging, wrinkled body. They'd found a four-family house in Astoria, just off Ditmars Boulevard. It seemed perfect—a kitchen, living room, three bedrooms, reasonable neighborhood, good shopping, close to Manhattan. Rent was three fifty-five, steep but not impossible. The landlady was a nasty bitch, but so what? They were ideal tenants—quiet, no children, income guaranteed by the U. S. government. They signed a three-year lease.

Al and Willie's fears about group living had not materialized. The benefits of steady companionship, of mutual care, outweighed the minor loss of privacy. When one man was cranky or irritable, the others learned to leave him alone. When one was sick, the others helped take care of him. They went to movies together, sat in Astoria Park together, accompanied each other to the mailboxes in the hallway, and then to the bank. Once Joe had brought a woman up to the apartment, but she hadn't stayed overnight. For the most part, things went quite well . . . until the economy soured.

In the mid-1970's a crazy thing happened—simultaneous unemployment and wild inflation. The Arabs cut off oil. Fertilizers, which require oil for various steps in their manufacture, skyrocketed in price. Which led to increased costs for grains. Which led to meat shortages, and made beef unaffordable for great numbers of Americans. Farmers were killing their chickens because they could not absorb the cost of feeding them. There was a depression, yet prices did not come down. Those who suffered most were those living on fixed incomes.

Joe, Willie, and Al found themselves living on pasta. "Spaghetti for breakfast, lunch, and supper," Al complained. "My body is starting to look like a

9

noodle." The movies had to be eliminated; even at senior-citizen rates the prices were too high. Once again, the old men found themselves scrimping on medicines, wearing clothing till it had holes in it, not running the exhaust fan even on hot summer nights. When the new lease came up, the landlady wanted four hundred twenty-five dollars a month. "And I can get it," Mrs. Flaum had snapped. "If not from you, then somebody else. I got people waitin' for this place." They'd signed a two-year renewal. Their social security payments were now two hundred thirty-seven dollars a month, an increase of about ten percent over three years earlier. During that time, of course, the cost of living had risen thirty percent. Even pasta was becoming a luxury. On the night the men shared their first package of dogfood, eating quickly and ashamedly in glum silence, Joe found himself unable to sleep.

A couple of the day's events had stimulated him so much that he lay wide awake in his bed, tossing uncomfortably in the darkness. He felt righteous anger. He was seventy-eight years old, had worked hard all his life, had never accepted welfare. If society was going to reduce him to living like an animal, eating an animal's food, he would retaliate. Someone, somewhere, he knew, was making a bundle on his misery. He felt this to be a law of economics—average wealth remained constant. Increases in productivity were offset by increases in population. If some bastards were raking it in, piling up profits, it was because he, Joe, and people like him, were on the verge of starvation. Time for us to get ours, he thought. Old is not dead. At least not yet.

After an hour and a half, he climbed out of bed, walked through the darkened hallway, and entered the kitchen. He flicked on the light and scanned the small counter for a pencil. His mind was whirring like an eggbeater. Why not? he thought. Desperate people have always taken desperate actions. The operative principle was: *Nothing to lose*. It was the idea behind murders and revolutions. Besides, thought Joe, this has an advantage. This will be fun. He located a tiny stub of a pencil, sharpened it to an irregular point with a kitchen knife, and sat down at the table. He retrieved the *Daily News* from the trash pail and placed it in front of him. This was the second time this newspaper had been removed from the garbage; Al had found it that morning in a waste basket in Astoria Park. The men referred to that particular basket as the "newsstand," since it was their primary source of newspapers. Joe carefully wrote the multiplication example in the margin: 237 x 36.

He mumbled as he worked out the answer; 8532. He grinned. He checked his work, stood up, and sat back down. "Eight thousand five hundred thirty-two dollars," he said aloud. He replaced the pencil stub on the counter, shut out the light, and started back toward the bedroom. Although it was still early September, the night was chilly; Joe, dressed in shorts and sleeveless undershirt, should have been cold. But the figures had left him pleasantly warm. His mind burned with a thousand plans and calculations and fantasies. He returned to his bed, not to sleep but to dream.

●　●　●　●

Al poured the steaming water, and the coffee crystals dissolved to a rich brown liquid in Joe's cup.

Joe had gotten up an hour earlier than usual; already he was showered, shaved, and dressed. Normally he strung these activities out slowly, a way of using time, making the day pass. But not today. Al gently pushed the cup toward him.

"Thanks," said Joe.

Al filled Willie's cup.

"Thanks," said Willie. He stared at the coffee a moment, then looked up. "Lemme have a little more water."

Willie was finicky. Sometimes after Al poured the water, Willie would add several more crystals of instant coffee to get the strength just right. Sometimes he'd actually *count out* the crystals.

"You want I should get an eyedropper?" said Al.

"Don't be a wise guy," said Willie. "Just pour."

Al gingerly tipped the ceramic pot.

"That's good!" said Willie quickly. "Perfect."

Al nodded, then filled his own cup. He put the pot back on the stove and returned to his seat. Joe and Willie added milk to their coffee; Al took his black. The three drank in silence. Today was not a "toast" day; the coffee would constitute their entire breakfast. Four days of the week, they allotted themselves one slice of white bread each. The remaining days were devoted, as Al put it, to "keeping trim."

"Must you sip so loud?" asked Al teasingly as Willie drank.

"Why, you got something better to hear?" said Willie. "This is my enjoyment."

"For your birthday I'll buy you a straw," said Al.

12

Joe smiled as he looked at them. "How you fellas feeling this morning?" he asked.

"What're you, a nurse?" said Al.

"Maybe he wants to take our temperatures," said Willie.

"Aw, come on," said Joe. "Give a guy a break. I was just interested in how my two best friends were doing."

"Well, I'm doing fine," said Al. "I'd be better if not for Willie's sipping, but I'm still pretty good."

"Willie?" said Joe.

"All right."

"Well, that's good to hear. Me, on the other hand, if I gotta spend another day doing nothing but sitting around in that park, looking at them ugly kids, I'm gonna go nuts." Joe pushed his cup away, and swallowed nervously before he voiced the idea that had kept him awake most of the night. "How'd you guys like to go on a stick-up with me?" he asked.

# 1
# Winners Either Way

The germ of the idea had generated spontaneously in the crushing boredom of the previous day. It began as a feeling, an intense desire for change, something to break the routine, no matter how good or bad or irrational.

The park where the three men were setting in spite of its openness, might as well have been a cage. The bench was their perch. And they themselves were tired denizens of an urban zoo, rotting away in captivity. Willie fed the pigeons with a piece of moldy bread he'd found in the garbage. Al read his *Daily News*. And Joe sat staring out into space. Behind them, children laughed and screamed as they ran through the shower of a water sprinkler. Young mothers rocked infants in carriages, talking about the price of meat, or their husbands' new jobs, or the start of school. It was 11:30 in the morning, and the old men had already been there for two hours.

Al lowered his paper and watched Willie dispense a chunk of bread to two scrawny birds. "How come you're always feedin' them, Willie?"

Willie shrugged. "They remind me a little of me. They're always here in the damn park. They toddle around without goin' anywhere. An' they're always hungry."

Al lifted his heavy eyebrows. "You know they say that they're supposed to bring disease."

"What disease? Cancer?"

"No, no, I don't know. I heard it somewhere."

"They never brought me no disease," said Willie.

Al nodded. "Look, don't get me wrong. I ain't one of those guys who got it in for pigeons. I—"

"You sound like it."

"No, no, I like the little buggers. It's nice havin' a little nature around here." Al paused. "I just heard they cause disease."

Willie broke off several chunks of bread in quick succession and scattered them around.

Al turned to Joe and elbowed him gently in the side. Joe nodded to indicate he understood: Al was not serious; Al was only teasing Willie to try to get a rise. It was an old story. Suddenly a fat three-year-old boy came running toward them, waving his pudgy arms and screaming. He thundered directly into the flock of pigeons that Willie had collected, and sent them flapping away violently in all directions. The men covered their faces as the cloud of crazed birds rose in the air, leaving a gradually settling residue of dust, dung, and feathers. The fat kid stood in front of the bench. It was as if he'd

16

jumped into a pool and all the water had splashed over the sides. He had a round, florid face and close-cropped hair. There was not a single aspect of his appearance that could be considered cute or endearing. He stared relentlessly at the three old men.

"What the hell's the matter with this kid?" said Joe.

The boy kept up his steady gaze. It was apparent, from the way his thick lips pinched together, that he found the men repellent. Al tried smiling gently, but the boy failed to respond. Food stains covered his fleshy face, and spilled onto his neck and shirt. The colors were red, yellow, and brown.

"If he eats any more jelly doughnuts," said Joe, "they're gonna have to take him to kindergarten in a moving van."

The boy continued to watch them curiously.

"They'll call him 'Tiny' when he grows up," said Al. "Hey Tiny, what's your name?"

The boy raised a buttery forearm and slapped at the air.

"Look at that mug," said Joe. "He's got one of them heads they make pisspots out of."

The boy's eyes narrowed.

"Do you believe the nerve this kid got?" Joe asked. He stood up. "Get the hell outta here!" he roared angrily.

With surprising fat man's speed, the boy scuttled hastily away. Joe shook his head and sat down. "Bugger!"

Al smiled. "Maybe he's going to get his father."

"From the looks of the kid, he'd need a building permit just to enter the park," said Joe.

"A little hard on the boy, weren't you?" said Willie.

17

"I don't enjoy bein' stared at like I'm some kind of exhibit," said Joe. "He wants to stare, let him go to a freak show or museum. There's such a thing as manners, you know."

Willie shrugged, and began again to distribute bread. The pigeons were returning.

"Too much excitement for one day," said Al, going back to his newspaper.

"I'm tellin' you," said Joe. He watched his two friends drift off into their own worlds. After a while he felt the muscles tighten in his jaw and a tension begin to build over his eyebrows. Why, exactly, was he feeling so angry? he wondered. And why so sad? Was it just an old man's summer melancholy, a wistful longing for more of life? Joe turned his face into the sun. He tried closing his eyes, thought maybe he'd doze off, but ten minutes passed and he was still awake. He stood up.

"I'm sick of this shit," he announced.

"What shit?" said Al, head still in the paper.

Joe swept his arm in front of him. "This. All of it."

Al looked up. "Beats getting hit in the head with a dull axe."

"Yeah?" said Joe. "I wonder about that." He looked over at Willie, who'd run out of bread. The pigeons, whose loyalty was minimal, had drifted away.

"Let's go home," said Joe.

"What time is it?" asked Willie.

"Time to go home," said Joe. "Checks are probably in by now."

They walked the four blocks back to their house, climbed the stoop, and entered the small

18

lobby. The remains of a broken lounge chair were heaped in one corner. Great hunks of ceramic tiles were missing from the floor. A torn, sun-browned curtain lay lankly against the glass portion of the door. Halfway up the right-hand wall was a row of rusting mailboxes. Joe fumbled with a tiny key, then inserted it in one of the locks. The metal panel squealed open, and he reached inside. Out came five envelopes. Joe kept three, handed one to Willie, another to Al.

"They're here," said Willie.

"What's your other two?" asked Al.

Joe opened the largest of his three envelopes. It contained a brochure advertising sexually oriented products. He thumbed through the pages while the others watched. Magazines with internal views of genitalia; sixteen-millimeter films featuring two women, women and beasts, two beasts; condoms with hundreds of spines, ridges, and tracks "to increase your partner's pleasure"; plug-in vibrators, battery-operated vibrators, vibrators that glowed in the dark, that had built-in FM radios; creams that got you hard, lotions that kept you hard, herbs that increased your staying power; devices for the kinky —electric wet suits, ben-wa balls, matching chain-whip-high-heel sets, stainless steel dildos; and finally, the books—*How to Make Slaves of Beautiful Women, Getting Girls Through Hypnosis, Thirty Things You Can Say That Will Drive a Woman Wild*.

"I like the last one," said Al. "Let's order it."

"I never said nothin' that drove a woman wild," said Willie.

"Who *wants* to drive a woman wild?" said Joe. "I jus' want 'em to lay down, that's all." He replaced the brochure in the mailbox. "Nice of 'em to send us this stuff, though. I guess they figured we'd be good customers."

The other men chuckled. "What's the last envelope?" asked Al.

Joe held it up. "Electric bill."

They headed for the bank. On the street, Joe ripped open the envelope. "You wanna see *real* pornography?" he said. "Here's real pornography."

Al glanced over his shoulder. "Jesus Christ."

"Forty-nine dollars!" said Joe. "For what? Who's using all the lights?"

"Don't look at me," said Willie.

The sun beat down steadily on the concrete. "Al?" said Joe.

"What?"

"Don't 'what' me. You know."

"I know what?"

"Every time you get up to take a leak at night, you forget to shut off the light in the bathroom."

"What are you talking about?"

"You heard me," said Joe. "I know. I'm up all hours."

"If you're up all hours," said Al, "you should know I don't even turn the light *on*."

"No wonder the seat's all wet in the morning," said Willie.

"Yeah?" coutered Al. "Well, at least I don't forget to flush."

Willie stopped. "Wait a minute. What are you trying to say here?"

"I'm not *trying* anything. I said it. You don't flush."

20

"That's ridiculous," said Willie. "I never forget that."

"You do."

"Don't." Willie hesitated. "Prove it."

Al guffawed. "You want evidence? You want me to save a sample and give it to the police crime lab?" He was rolling now. "Maybe you think it's like a bullet, that they can match it up to your particular rear end."

"All right," said Joe, coming between the two. "I'm sorry I brought it up already."

"He insulted me," pouted Willie.

"He had it coming," said Al.

"Let's forget about it, okay?" said Joe, and he resumed walking. "Nothing to start fighting about," he added. "It's only a couple of dollars."

"Couple here, couple there," said Willie. "Before long, you're broke."

At the bank they waited patiently on a long line. The air conditioning provided a relief from the outside heat. Joe's attention was caught by an armored truck that pulled up to the curb. As he watched, the rear of the truck opened, and two guards climbed out. A third guard began handing down canvas bags. An officer from the bank wheeled over a dolly, which was quickly filled to capacity. The officer and one guard pushed the dolly over to a special entrance adjacent to the front door and disappeared inside. A moment later, Joe saw them emerge behind the counter.

The line had moved up. Willie was already cashing his check. Joe nudged Al. "Get a load of all that dough."

"Yeah."

21

A male teller removed stack after stack of bills from one of the bags and placed the money in a large metal tray near his cage.

"I sure could put a dent in some of that," mused Al.

"You're telling me," said Joe.

"Next!" came a voice from behind the counter. Willie was standing off to one side. "Sir?" repeated the teller.

Al wrenched his gaze from the money.

"Sir, you're next."

Al's eyes remained glazed. "Al, wake up!" said Willie.

Al moved forward toward the counter, but Joe was still staring at the money.

● ● ● ●

For dinner they divided two-thirds of a chicken, and added some boiled potatoes. Dessert was Jell-O. The food was unsalted, in deference to Willie's high blood pressure. Afterward, Willie sat at the table reading someone's discarded *Post*, while Joe stared into his coffee and Al washed the dishes, singing loudly. First he sang "Sweet Adeline," and then, even louder, "That Old Gang of Mine."

Willie turned a page. "I see where Con Edison is asking for another increase," he said. "I think I'll learn to live in the dark."

There was a sharp knock at the door.

"Police," said Joe. "You know you ain't allowed to criticize the electric company."

Al stopped singing. "I'm all wet," he said, his hands immersed in soapsuds. "Can somebody get that?"

Willie folded his paper, shuffled to the door,

and undid the two locks. Before him stood Mrs. Flaum, the landlady. She was fifty-six years old, had her hair up in papered curlers, wore a raggedy smock, and stockings rolled down to the knees. There was a huge, hair-sprouting mole adjacent to her left nostril.

"Why, as I live and breathe," called Al from the sink. " 'Tis a vision of pure loveliness I see. I believe I died and went straight to heaven."

Willie stood sheepishly smiling, embarrassed by Al's mock praise.

"I . . . hello," he said awkwardly.

"What the hell do you think this is?" said Mrs. Flaum.

"I'm sorry, I—"

"You runnin' a cabaret up here?"

"No, no, uh—"

"I'm trying to live a life downstairs."

Al nodded and smiled. "I'm very sorry, Mrs. Flaum," he said. "I didn't realize how loud I was. Sometimes I get carried away." He bobbed his head. "It won't happen again."

"It *better* not happen again," said Mrs. Flaum. She peered over Willlie's shoulder into the kitchen. Something caught her attention, and she brushed past him into the apartment. It was not the first such visitation.

"Can we help you, Mrs. Flaum?" said Al sweetly.

The landlady ran her fingers over the stove top and came away with a thin coating of grease. "What is this?" she rasped. "Look at this."

"Just a little oil, Mrs. Flaum," said Al.

"Disgusting," she said. "This is really disgusting."

"We were just cooking on it," said Al. "We'll—"

"Don't you men ever clean up in here?" The landlady bent sightly to sniff her fingers and grimaced at the odor.

"Stove's been giving us fits," said Al. "Pilot light keeps goin' out."

Mrs. Flaum scowled. "By looking at this, you'd think a bunch of slobs live here." She stared at them. "Well?"

"We'll clean it right up," said Al. From the corner of his eye he noticed Joe sitting at the table, watching intently, his face rigid.

"You'd better," said Mrs. Flaum. The hairs on her mole stood straight out. "If you don't scour it all the time it gets so that you can never remove the filth. What do you think, I'm gonna buy a new stove for each new tenant?"

"Of course not, Mrs. Flaum," said Al.

"What do I tell the people after you?"

"Tell them there were three slobs used to live in the apartment," said Al, "but aren't there no more."

"You *won't* be there," said the landlady. "You read your lease. I got clauses coverin' things like this. The law is on my side."

"Of course it is," said Al. "We'll clean it right up."

"That's right, you will."

"We will."

Mrs. Flaum started for the door, which Willie hastened to hold open. She spun around. "And no more of that singing!"

"No more singing," said Al.

Mrs. Flaum stepped halfway out the door. "Okay, then."

24

"Good night, Mrs. Flaum," said Willie.

The landlady placed her hands on her hips and glared. "What are you trying, to rush me off my own property?"

"No," said Willie. "I was just saying good night."

She eyed him suspiciously. "You were, huh?"

"Yes."

"Because the lease gives me rights to perform inspections, ya know, if there's a reasonable presumption of damage to the premises."

"There's no damage," said Al. "You needn't worry your pretty head about that."

Mrs. Flaum watched him darkly. "All right. Good night then, gentlemen."

"Good night, Mrs. Flaum," said Al cheerfully.

Willie shut the door behind her and waited quietly, hearing her footsteps on the stairs. "Bitch," he said after a moment.

"I swear," said Al, "that woman's got eighty-eight teeth."

"If they threw her in a tank of piranha," said Willie, "it'd be the fish you'd see jumpin' over the sides."

"I'd like to try the experiment," said Al.

Willie shook his head. "I was a fool," he said. "I should've bought a house right after the war when I had the chance."

"Hindsight," said Al. "If you was to kick yourself for all the things you shoulda done, you'd wear your legs out." He paused a moment, aware suddenly that Joe hadn't spoken in nearly five minutes. It was unlike him to tolerate Mrs. Flaum's intrusion without even a single word. Al walked to the table. "Joe?"

Joe slowly lifted his eyes. "Yeah?"

"You all right?"

"Yeah, I'm okay."

"You sure?"

"You want a doctor's note?"

Al shrugged. "I noticed you ain't been eating too much lately. That could be a sign of something."

"Like poverty," said Willie.

Joe's attention seemed to drift. "Just haven't had an appetite," he mumbled.

Al and Willie exchanged glances, then Al returned to the sink. He rinsed the last glass, dried his hands, and headed into the living room to turn on the TV. Willie lingered behind with Joe. After awhile, Joe's eyes seemed to refocus. "What?" he said.

"Nothing," said Willie.

"Something's on your mind."

"No, no. It's just—you sure you're okay?"

"Yeah," said Joe. "Just thinking about things, that's all. You kow."

Willie nodded. He went into the living room. Al was turning the dial on the old 1956 RCA television. Al was the only one who could operate it properly, since the tuner was worn and the channels did not come in where they were marked. Al had the knack of stopping the dial at the right point and then using the fine-tuning to bring in the picture. An image appeared halfway between channels nine and ten.

"Leave this," said Willie.

"Leave what?" said Al, still working to clarify the picture. "You don't even know what it is yet."

"Let's see it," said Willie who was enthusiastic about anything that moved on the screen. Al found this lack of discrimination very irritating.

26

"C'mon, Willie. This is a rerun."

Willie sat down in the chair. "It looks good."

"We must've seen this a thousand times already."

"What're you talking about?" said Willie. "We ain't seen this once."

"Willie, I'm tellin ya—"

"Sit down, I can't see."

"We saw this already.

"Never."

"Don't you remember?" said Al. "They build a giant robot monster to fight the real monster, and the two of them battle it out just outside Tokyo."

"And who wins?"

Al looked at the ceiling. "The real one wins."

"He don't," said Willie. "See? You're thinkin' of somethin' else."

"Willie, I'm telling you, we saw this."

"Nope."

Al puffed out his cheeks. "You goin' senile on me now?"

Willie fell silent for a moment, then looked at him coldly. "Yeah, that's it."

"Hey, I was only—"

"Go ahead, change the damn channel."

"Aw, c'mon, Willie, I was just kiddin'."

"That's all right," said Willie, his voice still cold. "Change it."

"Willie—"

"Go ahead. Turn the knob. We saw this a thousand times, right?"

Reluctantly, Al moved the tuner. He hadn't wanted to hurt Willie's feelings, but there was little to do now. Willie *was* beginning to get senile, and he knew it, and was touchy about it. Al resolved not to tease him on that subject any more. There were plenty of other things to tease him about, after all. Between channels eleven and twelve an old gangster movie came on.

"Ooh, leave this," said Willie. "This is good."

Al fine-tuned the picture, then took a seat. The characters in the movie were on their way to rob a bank. He sat back and watched.

In the kitchen, Joe had shut off the light. Alone in the darkness, his attention was caught suddenly by snippets of dialogue that drifted in from the living room.

"All right, everybody! This is a stick-up! Everyone down on the floor!"

". . . small bills, only, you hear? Tens and twenties."

"Anyone moves for the next five minutes, they get their heads blowed off!"

Joe stood up and moved to the doorway. The light from the TV filled the kitchen with strange, flickering shadows. He studied the screen. Four gangsters were collecting sacks of money from frightened bank tellers. Guns blazing, the thieves exited the bank just as a black getaway car pulled up in front. As the men dived inside, the car jerked forward. A moment later, its brakes shrieking, it disappeared around a corner.

A commercial came on for an amazing vegetable processor that could cut in five different ways and would make a hit of any party. It sold for nine-ninety-nine and was available only from a special number in New Jersey. Joe retreated into the kitchen and sat again in the dark. His mind was going faster than even the fabulous chopper.

• • • •

"What was that again?" asked Al at the breakfast table the next morning.

"I said," said Joe carefully, "how's about we all go on a stick-up?"

Willie looked at him blanky; Al began to smile. After several seconds, Joe smiled back. "It's foolproof."

"That's what half the guys in Sing Sing said," noted Al.

"Different story entirely," said Joe. "With this, even if we lose, we win."

Al wrinkled his eyebrows. His wire-rimmed spectacles nearly fell off his nose.

"Look," continued Joe, "if the job works, we'll be in great shape. If not, maybe they'll give us three years . . . maybe . . . and that would be free room and board."

"Three years could be a life sentence," said Willie.

"Could be," agreed Joe. "But if not, when we get out we'd each have thirty-six Social Security checks waiting for us. And that, by the way, adds up to eight thousand, five hundred and thirty-two bucks . . . apiece." He looked around, as if proud of the calculation. "Not a bad hunk of change."

"That *is* a lotta dough," agreed Al. "You checked your numbers?"

"I did."

"You could buy a lotta meat with that kind of money," said Willie. "And I don't mean dogmeat, either."

"Or you could invest it," said Joe. "Maybe we could put all our dough together and buy one of

29

them newspaper and candy stands in some big Manhattan building. A friend of mine's son bought him one, and he lives pretty good. But what the hell are we talking about this for? Investments are only if we get caught . . . and I don't think we will be."

Willie was looking at him queerly.

"Well?" said Joe.

"Well, what?" said Willie.

"Well, what do you guys think?"

Al's face compressed itself in a tight smile. "I dunno. Sounds like a great idea."

"Willie?"

Willie turned to Al. "What do you mean, it sounds like a great idea?"

"I mean it sounds like a great idea."

"I don't understand," said Willie to Joe.

"Don't understand what?"

"I don't understand what you're talking about. Are you talking about actually doing this, or what?"

"Yeah . . . actually doing this," said Joe.

"Wait a minute," said Willie. "Just hold on there. I'm confused. Do you hear what you're saying?"

"Look," said Joe, "let me tell you something. I gotta think back and say my life was okay. I got my share of everything but money, and the guys that went out for that, some of them got it today but they put too much time in getting it. People forget that part. Whatever . . . that's history."

"Get to the point," said Al.

"It's coming," said Joe. "It's coming. Right now, here we are and I ain't complaining, but things would be a lot easier if we had a little extra cash. You agree so far, Willie?"

"Yeah," said Willie reluctantly.

30

"And besides," went on Joe, "what the hell is there for us to lose? Either we get the money, or we get caught. We're winners either way."

He looked at Willie triumphantly, confident his logic was impeccable. Willie would hem and haw and bitch a little, but he would come around.

Of course, Joe thought he had omitted perhaps the most compelling argument of all, the one that could not be measured in dollars and cents. Working on this project would relieve the deadly terminal boredom, would restore the sense of themselves as human beings instead of dried-out, mindless husks waiting to take their place among the fossils. This was the true worth of the idea, the real reason it was irresistible. Oh, Willie would stir up a fuss, Joe knew, but in the end he'd choose life. Past a certain age, conventional morality simply no longer applied. Willie would come to understand that, Joe thought. He'd have to.

# 2
# Family Album: Joe

It's 1901. Baby Joey Harris lies in the maternity ward at Bellevue, eight pounds six ounces of shriveled, bald, grasping, sucking half-Irish American. Three days later he's home, a tenement on Ninety-sixth Street, two rooms, occasional hot water. He grows up with Italians and Jews, raises a little hell, has his knuckles rapped in school. His parents are hardworking, uneducated, dedicated to their only son; they take him sledding in Central Park, touring around the Museum of Natural History, swimming at Coney Island. He graduates high school, gets a job as a clerk at the Five-and-Dime. There is no money for college, and besides, his grades aren't that good. He joins the Army, fights in the First Big One, is gassed in France, recovers.

It's 1922. Spats are in, skirts are short, and

young Joseph Harris is having a hot time. By day he sells shirts in a dry-goods store on Third Avenue; at night he does the Charleston, Black Bottom, and Heebie-Jeebie. Once he wins a marathon in Flatbush, collects a hundred dollars for dancing forty hours straight. Each new year brings a substantial salary raise. "The business of America is business," declares President Coolidge. Illegal liquor is plentiful, jazz is sweeping the country, and a young man named Ernest Hemingway writes a book called *A Farewell to Arms*. Joseph, not normally a reader, reads that one, and at the end, he weeps.

It's 1929. Joe meets Myrna Sawyer at a dance in the Bronx. She is shy and retiring, an old-fashioned girl who likes to cook and stay at home. A year later they are married. The stock market crash is a good buying opportunity, Joe decides. It's a temporary phenomenon, will last six months at the most; he invests his entire savings, fourteen hundred dollars. In 1934, the dry-goods store lays him off. Without cash, he is forced to sell his stock.

"Time to unload the Finley Shoes," he tells the broker.

The broker shakes his head. "Finley's went bankrupt four months ago," he says. He explains how the first call on assets went to the outside creditors, the remainder to the bond holders and owners of preferred shares. "There's nothin' left for those who've got the common stock," he adds.

Joe peddles underwear and socks on the street. When it rains, he sells umbrellas; when winter comes, he pushes gloves and knit caps. In bad years he even tries to move a few Christmas trees; if the people aren't buying, he shovels snow. He and Myrna move into a tiny apartment in the Bronx, one room, no running water. As for Home Relief, the hell with that, says Joe. He'll be damned if he'll stand in those long, sad lines with his palm out. A *man* just doesn't do that sort of thing.

In 1941 America finally enters the war. Joe works in a factory on Long Island. His job is to bend sheet metal for the wings of airplanes, and there's as much overtime as a man could want. He puts in sixteen hours daily until V-J Day, loses partial hearing in one ear as a result of the constant noise, forfeits half a pinky in an accident with a saw. He is disgusted with the work; on impulse, one sunny spring Friday afternoon, he gives two weeks' notice. He is unemployed for three months, then finds a job in Queens, selling ladies' clothing. He, Myrna, and the kids move to a garden apartment in Forest Hills, a mile from where he works.

The business does well; Joe can charm the women into anything. He himself, of course, is charmed into purchasing an overpriced car, a dining room set, a couch that seats five. By 1950, he has a son, Brian, in high school, and two girls, in junior high. When the Korean War breaks out, Brian rushes to join the Navy, but is rejected because of his health. The physical examination reveals an early form of diabetes.

At the store, Myerson, the owner, calls Joe aside one day; Myerson is getting old, wants to sell half the business, would Joe be interested in buying? Joe has some money now, could possibly borrow the rest, but nevertheless declines the offer. "Who needs the headache?" he says to Myrna. Another salesman, who came in after Joe, decides to take the plunge. The business goes so well he opens a second store, skips over Joe for manager. That's the way it goes, says Joe. I *still* ain't sorry.

In 1969, Joe retires. He is sixty-eight years old. Brian works in Los Angeles for Columbia Pictures. The youngest girl, Jean, lives in Miami; Betty, the middle daughter, is with the Peace Corps in Uganda. Joe hardly sees them. After Myrna dies in 1971, they all pledge to keep in touch, get together more frequently—but, somehow, it doesn't happen. Once Joe takes a bus trip out to California, visits Brian in his small, suburban ranch house. His three grandchildren are polite and friendly but, of course, hardly know him. Brian and his wife are having some kind of marital problem; by the time a week passes, Joe senses his presence has increased the strain. He leaves; now he and his only son lose touch.

In 1979, Joe is seventy-eight years old. His spine is beginning to curve, his cheeks to sink beneath the bones of his face, his shoulder and hip joints to freeze. But he still has all his hair, even if it is a bleached-out white, and he still has an infectious, mischievous smile. His income from Social Security is two hundred thirty-seven dollars a month.

# 3
# The Goats in the Basement

They walked down Ditmars Boulevard, the warm September sun beating down from directly overhead. As usual, Joe was out in front, Willie and Al dragging slightly behind.

"I did some stealing during the war," said Joe, "so I'll set everything up."

"What do you mean, 'you did some stealing'?" said Al. "I thought *I* was the only experienced thief around here." Al had years before worked as a bartender; during Prohibition, he'd smuggled some booze. His involvement was actually quite minor, but you'd never know it from his stories. "And what war?" he asked Joe now.

Joe grinned. In World War I, he'd been with a company that had occupied a small German town near the French border. Joe and a few friends had bought cartons of cigarettes from the base PX and resold them to the German burghers at four times the price. The transaction was conducted in a tent pitched on an unpaved side street; Joe would do the actual bargaining. When the customer emerged and had gone a few blocks, Joe's friends would arrest him and seize his belongings. "Black market cigarettes," they'd say, when they found the cartons. "We'll have to take these, they're illegal." The cowed customer would slink away, and the cigarettes would be returned to the tent. The men managed to sell the same goods eight times before word finally got around.

"Never mind what I mean," Joe told Al now. Why tell them that his only experience with stealing was completely irrelevant to what they wanted to do? Why worry them? After all, he had seen his share of crime movies, and had avidly followed the doings of Capone and Lepke and Dillinger in the papers. Besides, what was there to know?

He recognized a tall, graying woman approaching them on the street. "Hello, Mrs. Spelios."

Mrs. Spelios nodded. "How are all of you feeling today?"

Willie tilted his head. "Well, you know, the bursitis is—"

Joe poked him in the side. "We're very good, thank you. And yourself?"

"Don't ask," said Mrs. Spelios. "God's curse is to be old."

"A shame," said Joe, without sympathy. "I hope things will improve."

"Never," she said.

"See you later," said Joe.

"Ya," said Mrs. Spelios. "If I'm still alive."

"Good-bye," said Al.

She passed them and continued on.

"Why'd you poke me?" Willie asked Joe.

"Why? Because if you tell her one thing is wrong with you, she tells you twenty things wrong with her. You got a little bursitis, she'll give you a half-hour spiel on her heart murmurs, and her hysterectomy, and her arthritis in her hands, and her root canal work, and even her athlete's foot. You can't win with that woman. Even if you're dead, she's worse. Last week she cornered me for an hour, told me about some yeast infection in her vagina. Most disgusting thing I ever heard. I'm seventy-eight years old, I don't want to know from that."

"I think it's interesting," said Willie.

"I'll tell you what's interesting," said Joe. "We're gonna need some guns."

Willie stopped walking. "I don't believe this."

"Willie," said Joe patiently, "we're gonna need your help, we can *use* your help . . . but if you don't wanna go, that's okay too."

"I haven't said definitely—"

"I respect your feelings," said Joe. "I'm sure Al does too. Al, is that right?"

"Yeah, I respect his feelin's," said Al. "I don' understand 'em, but if that's what he wants to do—fine."

"I'm just not sure yet," said Willie. "I mean the idea of three old men . . ."

"I want you to know," said Joe solemnly, "that you'll still be our partner and we'll cut you in on everything. That is, if it's okay with Al, of course."

"Yeah, it's okay with me," said Al. "I don' understand it, but if that's what you think is right—then fine."

"Yeah?" said Willie. "And if you go to jail, am I still gonna be your partner?"

"Through thick and thin," said Joe. "For better or worse."

"I hear they got a lot of them homos in jail," said Willie.

"Yeah, maybe. So what?"

"I'm afraid of gettin' raped."

"You won't get raped. Who wants old coots like us?"

Willie shook his head, and they resumed walking.

"My nephew Pete is a gun nut," said Al. "He's got a little collection he keeps in a cabinet down in his basement."

"Well?" said Joe.

"So maybe there's somethin' for us."

"When can you find out?"

"I'm going over there to watch his kids for a little while this afternoon."

"Sounds good."

"Soon's I have a chance," said Al, "I'll go down and check everything out."

"Great," said Joe. "But remember, don't say nothing to nobody."

"Of course not," said Al. "I'm not a *complete* fool, am I?"

"No one's perfect." Joe turned to Willie and put an arm around his shoulder. Willie's face was pinched with tension. "Don't be torturin' yourself now," said Joe. "It's not worth it, and it's not necessary."

"It *is* necessary," said Willie. "I never stole nothing in my life."

"But the government steals from *you*," said

40

Joe. "And they been stealin' all along. I mean, is it right that an old man who worked so many years ends up havin' to eat dogfood for dinner? Where's the morality in that?"

"It ain't the government's fault we're poor," said Willie.

"It *is*," insisted Joe. "All these years they been printin' money like it's going out of style. The mint's in the business of makin' paper, an' so you got all these dollar bills floatin' around buying up cars and lettuce and sweaters. Naturally, the prices hit the moon. If you got a job, you tell the boss you need a raise. But if you're like us, you're stuck."

"We tell our congressman," chimed in Al, "only he's too busy gettin' *his* to worry much about ours."

"Sure, now an' then they throw the old folks a bone," said Joe. "Usually it takes one of them nursin' home fires, or some poor couple found starved or somethin'—and then people remember for a little while. Oh yeah, we forgot about the *elderly*, they say. Yeah, let's raise the Social Security by another two percent. And that's the way it goes till the next tragedy."

Willie compressed his lips. "It's still stealin'," he said, "no matter how you justify it or talk around it."

"Sure, it's stealin'," said Joe. "I never said it wasn't. As for justifyin'—all I claim is that people our age gotta look out for themselves. Nobody's gonna do it for 'em."

Willie nodded uncertainly.

"Don't worry about a thing," reassured Joe. "We're gonna make you feel young again."

It was an old, small house in Jackson Heights; every five minutes a plane landing at LaGuardia Airport would buzz the roof.

Kathy, Pete's wife, met her husband's uncle at the door. "Colleen and Kevin are inside," she said. "I told them you were coming, and I left them something to eat, so everything should be fine."

"Yeah, yeah, don't worry," said Al. "I can handle everything at this end. You stay as long as you like."

Kathy leaned over and kissed him on the cheek. "You're really a sweetie pie," she said. "I'll be back in about an hour. In emergency, if you have to reach me, I'll be at Queens General Hospital, visiting Rita Dolan. Number's on the table."

"We'll be fine," said Al. He walked inside. Passing through the small living room, he stopped just outside the kitchen doorway and peeked around the edge. A girl and boy were sitting at the table. The boy, age seven, was picking listlessly at a sandwich. His face was serious, intent; his long hair came down almost over his eyes. The little girl, age three, seemed more relaxed. She was eating something from a plastic bowl. *Her* hair was a disorganized mass of tight curls. Suddenly, as Al watched, the boy leaned over and took something from the girl's bowl. She screamed.

"Mommy said you're not supposed to!"

"I can if I want," declared the boy

"No, you're not finished!"

"I *am.*"

"No." The little girl screamed again. "Give it back!"

"I ate it already," said the boy.

The girl, who had seemed unaware of Al's pres-

42

ence, was not; she now addressed him directly. "Mommy said he mustn't take any potcorn until he finishes," she said.

Al entered the kitchen.

"Hi, Uncle Al," said Kevin.

"Hello, Kevin," said Al. "Hello, Colleen." He walked to the table and kissed the little girl. The boy, he knew, would not tolerate such open affection.

"He's a bad boy," said Colleen, pointing to Kevin.

"Why is he bad?" said Al.

"He . . . he don't eat his fish," said Colleen.

"I do!" said Kevin. "She's a liar. She has to share."

"Mommy said: if he don't eat, he can't have potcorn," said Colleen.

"She means *pop*corn," said Kevin. "And I ate more than half my fish."

"How about if he has a few pieces," said Al to Colleen, "bein' that he did eat half?" He tickled her neck and the girl squealed in laughter.

"Okay," she said. "But you have to get me orange drink."

Al nodded. He gave Kevin some popcorn from Colleen's bowl, then went to the refrigerator and took out a half-gallon container of orange drink. He poured some in a plastic cup for each child. "There," he said, bringing the cups to the table, "that wasn't so hard to solve, was it?" He felt quite satisfied with himself.

"Except she always gets me in trouble," said Kevin.

"I do *not*," said Colleen.

"She stinks!" said Kevin.

"No-oo-oo-oo!" Colleen began to cry.

"Shhh!" said Al. "Everyone shhh!" When the racket abated a little, he cooed, "Now . . . Uncle Al has to go down to the basement for a few minutes. When I come up, if you're not good, you'll each get hit in the head."

Kevin smiled.

"Don't hit my head!" yelled Colleen.

"Why not?" said Al.

"Because Mommy doesn't like me to get my hair messed," said Colleen.

"Well, then, you be a good girl," said Al. He crossed to the basement door, flicked on the light switch, and made his way down the wooden steps. At the bottom, on the right, he saw the mahogany gun cabinet where Peter, his nephew, kept his small collection. He ran his hand along the top of the cabinet until his fingers closed on a key. Quickly, he unlocked the top drawer and then the ones beneath it. Al knew that periodically Pete went hunting, and occasionally target shooting; it was Al, in fact, who'd helped him build the cabinet. But as to what was *in* the cabinet, Al had no idea. Rifles would be of little use. They were clumsy and conspicuous to transport, difficult to handle for close range use, relatively easy to trace.

The bottom two drawers contained rifles. The third drawer was filled with ammunition, perhaps ten different boxes of bullets of various caliber. Al slid open the top drawer. He stared for a moment. Inside, resting on a blue velvet cloth, were four pistols. Al slid the drawer shut, made sure all the locks were closed, then replaced the key on top of the cabinet. He went back upstairs.

Kevin had the Lotto cards distributed on the table.

"I didn't hear any noise, so you must've been good," said Al. He noticed that all the popcorn was gone.

"We *were* good," said Colleen

"What were you doing in the basement?" asked Kevin.

"Looking for ghosts," said Al.

Kevin grinned. "There's no such thing."

"Sure there are," said Al.

"Nah."

"Yes. I thought I heard one. That's why I went down there."

Kevin's grin changed gradually to a look of concern. "And was there one there?"

"How could there be?" teased Al. "There's no such thing as a ghost."

"You mean goats?" said Colleen. She smiled broadly, her eyes gleaming, delighted chortles gurgling from her cherub lips. "There's no goats in the basement."

Al nodded. "You're right," he said. "Uncle Al was just teasing." But Kevin, he noticed, was no longer quite so sure.

● ● ● ●

Kathy had been nearly an hour late getting back, and then Al had to wait almost thirty minutes for the bus to Astoria. Younger people always assumed that waiting was easier for old folks, he reflected. That the elderly, because they had no job to rush off to, or children to feed, somehow didn't mind aimless, mindless periods of doing nothing. That bank lines and bus lines and the benches of health clinics were their natural habitat. Of course, it wasn't

45

true. Waiting was as boring for the old as the young; the former were simply not as vocal in their resentment. It was past 4:30 in the afternoon when Al entered Astoria Park.

Two teen-agers approached him. One wore a vest with no shirt underneath; his pony tail reached two feet down his back. The other, in bandana and T-shirt, had the bulk and muscle of a wrestler. On his shoulder was a tattoo: SEX KILLS.

"Hey, Pop, you got a cigarette?" said the ponytail.

Al kept on walking.

The teen-ager stopped, then turned back. "Hey, man, I asked you something!"

Al kept going. He felt a hand on his shoulder.

"Hey, it's not polite not to answer," said the wrestler. "My friend asked you a question."

"Take your hand off my shoulder," said Al.

The boy did not move. Al brought his own wrist up suddenly and knocked the hand off. The boy quickly replaced it. "We got a tough egg here," he laughed to his friend.

"You'd better let me alone," said Al. He tried to resume walking, but the hand on his shoulder tightened like a steel pliers.

"*First*, you answer the question," said the wrestler.

"I didn't hear," said Al. The pain was beginning to spread to his chest.

"You heard," snarled the ponytail.

"I didn't."

"He says he didn't hear," said the ponytail.

The bulky boy increased the pressure. The pain was so paralyzing, Al could barely speak. "I . . .

46

don't . . . have any cigarettes," he croaked through clenched teeth.

"He don't have any," repeated the wrestler. The pressure eased.

"See?" said the ponytail. "All we wanted was some courtesy." He looked at Al through violent turquoise eyes. "How about lending me a dollar so's I could get some?"

"Go to hell," said Al. He backed away.

"Come on," said the wrestler, advancing. "A dollar ain't much."

Al knew another shoulder pinch would make his arm immobile for days. He looked around. The nearest people were a hundred yards away, what good would be an old man's hoarse screams? Besides, there was the embarrassment. . . . Slowly, pain streaking down his arm, he reached into his pocket. He threw the dollar bill at the ponytail's feet. "You should be ashamed," he said.

The boy bent to pick up the money. "I ain' ashamed of nothin'!" he snapped.

"Someday," said Al. "You wait. Someday, you'll be old."

The boys smiled at each other, and walked jauntily away. Al stood motionless for several minutes. At last he managed to reach around and massage the soreness in his shoulder. Bastards, he thought. Sonofabitch criminal bastards. He began to cry with frustration and humiliation. "Twenty years ago I would've killed those punks," he said aloud. What good is it what you would've done, he thought. Twenty years ago, they weren't alive. The only thing that matters is today and tomorrow. The past is a mirage in an old man's mind, an image on a fading film, a ghost in the basement. He dried the tears from his cheeks and hurried along.

• • • •

Joe and Willie were sitting on their usual bench. Before them three little boys were playing cowboys-and-Indians. Two of the boys had toy pistols, while the third simply imagined a gun out of a forefinger and raised thumb. There was a great deal of shooting at point-blank range, although no one seemed to actually die.

"Hey, I got you!" a blond boy protested to the gunless cowpoke.

"You did not."

"I did! Right between the eyes. You're dead!"

"I am not."

"Are."

"Not."

"Are." The blond appealed to Joe. "Mister, isn't he dead?"

Joe looked at him. "He don't look dead to me."

"No, I mean, didn't I get him with my gun?" whined the boy.

"He did not," said the thumb-and-forefinger cowboy. He hesitated, weakening in the face of the blond's determination. "Maybe he wounded me," he admitted. "I think I ducked and he wounded me." He held his arm limply.

"How could I wound you in the arm if you ducked?" asked the blond logically. "Make believe I shot off the top of your head . . . but you're still alive."

"I don't want to be shot in the head," protested the other boy.

"Then you're chucked," said the blond. He turned to the third boy, who was a bit older than the other two. "If he's not wounded in the head, he can't play, right?"

"Right," agreed the older boy.

The gunless cowpoke moaned, but accepted his fate. "Well, make believe I wear a hat," he said, "so you can't *see* that part of my head is off."

This seemed a reasonable compromise. The game resumed.

"See," said Joe, "they're like us. They have differences, they work them out."

"They're not planning a robbery," said Willie.

"They're dealing with guns," said Joe. "And they actually use theirs. Ours will be just for show."

"Unless something goes wrong," said Willie.

"Nothing *can* go wrong," said Joe. "What are we, crazy? We agreed, there's no way we can come out on the short end here."

"There's always risk. What if someone shoots us? I'd call that a short end. And your hat won't cover the hole in your head, either."

"Willie," said Joe, "there's risk when you cross the street. At least, like this, we'll be makin' our future, not leaving it to chance. Ain't you tired of thinking that you always got your finger on the action just because of the two bucks you throw away each month on them lottery tickets?"

Willie grinned. "It supports education."

"Okay," said Joe, not cracking a smile. "Well, then think how much more you can contribute from your share of the take."

"Bet you didn't know your friend was such a philanthropist, did you?" said Willie.

"It had escaped my notice," said Joe.

A fourth little boy had charged onto the grass in front of them. He was wearing an Army helmet and, weaponless, he was pretending he had a machine gun. With rapid eh-eh-eh-ehs, he sprayed the other players with a barrage of bullets. Their potency was evidenced by all his targets sinking to the ground. When Joe looked up, Al was sitting alongside him.

"What's going on?" Al asked.

"Massacre," said Joe. "Soldier killed the cowboys and Indians. Superior technology, looks to me." He paused. "And what about our own armaments?"

Al rubbed the shoulder where it still hurt. The pain had subsided to a dull, deep ache. "It's perfect," he said. "No problems."

"What'd you find?" asked Joe.

"Four pistols. There are these four pistols right in the top drawer. We don't want rifles, right?"

"Right."

"'Cause Pete got a couple rifles too."

"No rifles."

"All right," said Al. "There are these four pistols. One of them is a German machine type. Seemed a little heavy. I didn't think it'd be too good."

"And the others?"

"Thirty-eights, I think. The other three looked great." He winced as his finger prodded an inflamed area that seemed to extend to his neck.

"Bursitis actin' up?" asked Joe. "Mine's been killin' me."

"Nah," said Al. "Had a little run-in with some young punks when I come into the park. One of the little darlin's grabbed me by the shoulder an' spun me around."

"Bastards," said Willie. "Takin' advantage of an old man."

"Never mind," said Al. "Soon's I got my bearin's I scared hell out of 'em. You never seen kids run so fast. Twenty years ago I woulda chased after the little creeps and—"He stopped, conscious of their stares. "Anyway, the whole thing amounted to a heap of beans." He stopped rubbing his shoulder.

"Gettin' back to the guns," said Joe. "You think you'll have any problem sneakin' them out of there?"

"It'll be a piece of cake," said Al.

"When all this is over, we'll give your nephew some money, okay?"

"Okay with me," said Al.

"Willie?"

"May as well," said Willie. "One way or another *we* don't figure to be around to spend it."

"Just one other thing," said Joe. "If—I said 'if,' Willie—we happen to get caught, we don't tell where we got the guns, right?"

"Right," said Al. "Good point."

"You sure you wasn't in the Mafia?" said Willie.

"I taught the Godfather everything he knew," said Joe.

There was silence as the men drifted into their own streams of thought. The young mothers in the park began to collect their children. It was 5:15 in the afternoon, time to go home. Men would be returning from work soon and they'd be hungry, would want supper on the table. Only those people without families could afford to spend their lives on wooden benches.

"What're we gonna stick up?" asked Al suddenly.

"I was just thinkin' about that," said Joe.

"How about a liquor store," suggested Al.

"Oh, come on," said Willie. "Some poor guy spends twelve hours a day in his place, six days a week, tryin' to eke out a livin', an' you wanna hold him up? Forget it. A man puts his life savings in a store of his own, I ain't about to rob him. That's . . . that's criminal. Count me out." He turned away from the others.

"Willie," said Joe, "this is just a discussion here. We're brainstormin', tryin' to get a fix on things. We ain't actually *doin'* anything until we agree. You got a better place to rob, let's hear it. We got open minds."

Sullenly, Willie swiveled back. "How 'bout a department store?"

"Too hard," said Al, shaking his head. "First of all, they got security guards all around, and also hidden alarm systems. Second, the cash is in thirty different registers, too much to collect from. Third, there's too many people to be able to control. Fourth—"

"All right, all right," said Willie. "I get the point."

"Now, if you're talkin' holding up the payroll truck for a department store," said Al, "maybe you got a different story."

"That's not what I'm suggesting," said Willie.

"It would take too much planning," said Joe. "We'd have to follow the truck on its route, see when the guards break for coffee, stuff like that. And how can we follow the truck when none of us drives?"

"The whole thing is preposterous," said Willie.

"It just requires some thought," insisted Al. "Any worthwhile project needs planning."

Again, the old men lapsed into silence. The park was nearly empty now; the sounds of laughing children had stopped.

"A hijacking?" said Willie, after five minutes.

"A hijacking of what?" asked Al.

"I dunno. A plane?"

"We can't afford no plane tickets," said Joe.

"Something else, then," said Willie.

"What—a train?" said Al. "How about this: We get on one of them Metroliners and tell 'em to take us to Cuba."

Willie waved down Al's raucous laughter with a threatening motion of his hand.

Joe waited until the byplay had ceased. "Might as well make it a bank then, right?" he said with exaggerated sweetness.

"Yeah, I guess so," said Al, as if he'd been considering that possibility all along but had refrained from broaching it until all other ideas were exhausted.

"Willie," said Joe, "what do you think?"

"You're asking the wrong person," said Willie grumpily.

"Yeah . . . well . . . I think a bank would be pretty good," said Joe.

"As Willie Sutton once observed, 'That's where the money is,'" commented Al.

"I say, we might as well go all the way," continued Joe. "Banks are often lightly guarded, their funds are concentrated, and you can find times when there's hardly any people in 'em." He looked at Willie. "An' one very important thing is that no little guy ends up gettin' hurt. Banks are insured by the government for exactly the kind of thing we got in mind."

Willie tilted his head. "You wouldn't rob our own bank, would you?"

"Nah," said Al. "That would be foolish. Why pick one in the neighborhood? They know us here. Besides, if we succeeded, I'd lose all my confidence in them. I'd never deposit any more money."

"We'll take a ride into the city," said Joe. "We'll do it tomorrow. We can ride around the whole day. Must be a million banks there."

"Sounds good," said Al.

"To you, everything seems wonderful," said Willie. "If I said, 'Tomorrow, we all die of cancer,' you'd say, 'Sounds good.'"

"Sounds good," said Al.

Joe turned to Willie. "You gonna come along with us for the ride?"

Willie met his gaze for a moment before lowering his eyes. "Yeah . . . I'll come with you." He glanced up. "But no funny stuff!"

"None," said Al.

"Serious business only," said Joe.

The three men stood up. "I bought some cans of stew," said Willie.

"Forget stew," said Joe. "I say, tonight we eat out. We celebrate."

"Celebrate what?" asked Al.

"Our coming good fortune," said Joe.

Willie shrugged. "Suits me," he said. "I don't have to tell you what we'll be eatin' all next week, but if you guys wanna live it up tonight, I'm in."

"Okay," said Al. "Will it be 21 or The Four Seasons?"

"I'd prefer McDonald's or Burger King," said Willie.

"We'll compromise," declared Joe.

They settled on a White Castle.

# 4
# Family Album: Al

It's 1907, and Alan McGuinnes is born in Summer's Point, a small resort town in southern New Jersey. Business in his parents' luncheonette is not good that year and the number of free-spending vacationers is way below usual. Still, the family hangs on, and in the next years things get better. Al's father works seven days a week, and in 1910 manages to acquire a small, two-story house, which he converts to a hotel. The mortgage is small, and the family is able to make ends meet.

Amusements are simple: a short train trip for a day in Atlantic City, a walk on the beach, a perusal of the Sears Roebuck catalog. Alan learns to play the banjo and harmonica, does a great rendition of "Waiting for the Robert E. Lee." After school, he helps out in the luncheonette, jerking sodas, waiting tables. His idol is Ty Cobb, the famous baseball player. The major issues of the day—corrupt city governments, labor abuses, tariff policies—seem remote and unrelated to his life, although one day in 1919 a strange thing happens. A group of belligerent, sign-bearing women barge into the hotel and demand that Al's father stop serving wine at the small bar off the lobby. Al's father is at first amused, then irritated, and he attempts to throw the women out. There is a scuffle; eventually the women leave. Through it all, Al notices a very pretty young girl near the rear of the lobby. She is holding a sign but, looks passive and out-of-place. He observes that she seems uninterested in the proceedings; instead, she watches him.

Her name is Mary Doyle, and she and Al go together for four years. Al loves her. He tells her they will be married when he is eighteen, but in 1923 Al's father abruptly makes an announcement: They are moving to Florida. A feverish real-estate boom is under way. He has made a deal to purchase a luncheonette in Coral Gables; in the back, says Al's father with a laugh, are complete facilities for brewing now-illegal beer. Al is heartbroken. He and Mary say tearful good-byes, promise to write, to visit.

The move is made, and business is good. Coral Gables is the "American Venice," a subtropical middle-class paradise. The back room of Al's parents' store is expanded. Al is a singing waiter. He plays the banjo when Gilda Grey, the famed shimmy dancer, comes down from Chicago for a three-day booking. The homey luncheonette speakeasy grows increasingly successful; even millionaires from Palm Beach and Boca Raton come to visit to see what all the fuss is about. Occasionally, they and other customers throw Al money, but he refuses to pick it up. The owner's son doesn't take handouts, he thinks. Let the other waiters do that. Wine is added to the beverage list (Al's father mixes water with a processed grape jelly called Vine-Glo; after sixty days it is potently alcoholic), and then smuggled rum. Al sings, to the customers' amusement:

*Mother makes brandy from cherries;*
*Pop distills whisky and gin;*
*Sister sells wine from the grapes on our vine—*
*Good grief, how the money rolls in.*

And then, suddenly, it stops. One night, a certain rotund "millionaire" turns out to be wearing a disguise. He is actually Izzy Einstein, the famous Prohibition agent. During the raid that follows, the premises are reduced to rubble in an orgy of bottle breaking and furniture smashing. Under the provisions of the new Jones Act, passed in 1929, Al's father is fined five thousand dollars and sentenced to jail for three years. He dies in prison after four months. Al, however, has made a connection. The "businessmen" who furnished the smuggled rum from the Bahamas need people to transport it to New York. Al's mother and sisters have no income; it is up to Al to be the breadwinner. He makes fifty-four separate trips in three different Packards, their back seats and trunks bulging with bottled booze. Financially, he does quite well, especially considering that the country is in the Depression, and nearly everyone else is out of work. In 1933, however, the Twenty-first Amendment is passed. Prohibition is repealed, and the need for liquor smugglers is over.

Al is nevertheless able to connect again, this

time as a bartender at a Bronx speakeasy he former-
ly supplied. He has an outgoing personality, and the
customers like him. He has arm-wrestling and head-
butting contests with the patrons. The latter, in
which two men stand inside a painted circle with
their hands behind their backs and try to force each
other outside the boundary, become a big local
draw. Al's boss increases his salary. Al bets on himself, wins a little money. He brags: "I take these
popcorns for everything they're worth." This is
meant in more ways than one; Al is not averse to re-
lieving a thoroughly drunk customer of some extra
cash. Occasionally, he even steals from the cash register. After all, he thinks, I'm supporting my family,
and that comes first. In 1938, a Greek soccer player
butts Al unconscious and fractures his skull. Al's boss
pledges to rehire him when he comes out of the hospital, but does not keep his word.

Al doesn't worry. For a month he sells Christmas trees, then lands a bartending job at the Bilt-
more Hotel in Manhattan. He is still lovable, still a
free spender, still enjoys a good time. Twice a week,
after work, he and a bunch of friends make the
rounds of the whorehouses on MacDougal Street
in the Village. One day in 1943, Al spots a face that
is wrenchingly familiar.

"Mary?"

The woman, on her way to one of the bedrooms
with a john, tries unsuccessfully to hide.

"Mary Doyle?"

They talk. He asks why she stopped writing,
why she never answered his letters. She explains
how she met someone else, married when she was
seventeen, divorced, and married again. "He was
killed at Pearl Harbor," she says vacantly.

Al sees her a few times, but feels vaguely uncomfortable, and finally he breaks it off. The fact is, a lot of girls are crazy about him, and he is having too much of a good time to think about settling down with anybody. The metal plate in his head (from the butting accident) has made him ineligible for the Army; while America's young men are overseas defending the country, he will see to it that their women are kept happy. In 1952, a tiny article on page twenty of the *Mirror* catches his eye: *Prostitute Murdered in Village*. Al sees the name: Mary Doyle. Stabbed to death by a customer. His melancholia lasts for nearly a week.

Always, he is a ladies' man, but always he remains unattached. Photographs show him on city beaches—Orchard, Brighton, Coney Island—with a beauty on each arm. He bartends at many different hotels, many different restaurants. He is happy-go-lucky, a free spirit, "no permanent obligations," as he puts it. In 1979, Al is seventy two years old. He has high blood pressure, arteriosclerosis, and frequent headaches. He still has no permanent obligations. His income from Social Security is 237 dollars a month.

# 5
# The Glass Hill

Three Puerto Rican kids entered the car at the Thirty-sixth Avenue station and immediately set up shop near one of the doors. While the oldest, a teen-ager, knocked out a furious beat on a set of dilapidated bongos, the other two—a boy and a girl who appeared to be less than ten—did a frantic series of shimmies, tap steps, cartwheels and handsprings down the center aisle. Then the younger children made their way among the passengers, collecting the proffered coins.

"How old are you?" asked Al, when the boy stood in front of him.

The child had the honey-brown skin of the Caribbean Latin. He wore a loose, torn cotton shirt that exposed his dark, skinny chest, and one front tooth had been jaggedly broken off. He held up nine fingers.

"Nine?" Al said.

The boy nodded shyly.

"Barely older than Kevin," muttered Al. "You dance very well," he added loudly.

"Come on," Joe prodded, "give him his dough. He's waitin' to go to the next car."

Al, who had been groping in his pocket for a quarter, decided on a dollar. He put the bill in the boy's hand. Imagine if it *was* Kevin, he thought. Goin' through trains like this. . . . These kids probably don't eat if they don't get a certain amount of money.

"*Gracias, senor*," said the boy.

"You're a good lad," said Al. He reached out to pat the boy's head, but the child had already moved on.

"Probably make a fortune, those kids," said Joe, when the troupe had disappeared into the next car.

"There's the germ of Joe's next idea," said Willie. "The Three Dancin' Old Men. Al, you can play the ocarina, while me an' Joe does a soft-shoe in the aisles."

"Sounds good," said Al.

The subway train rocked and rumbled on its way to Thirty-ninth Avenue. It was late morning, past the rush hour, and not too many people were riding. The inside and outside of the car were covered with elaborate graffiti. Willie scanned the messages, which were mostly obscene insults, and was amazed, not by their subject matter but by the artistry with which they had been created. Giant red, blue, and yellow letters, painted by seemingly accomplished calligraphers, covered almost all the wall and ceiling areas. It seemed strange that such gifted artists chose to express only the most banal sentiments.

"Willie?"

"Wha?" Willie looked up as he felt Joe's elbow nudging him.

"It's great to be doing something, huh?"

Willie's expression remained pensive.

"Come on," chimed in Al. "Admit it."

Willie raised his eyebrows slightly. "All right, I admit it. But only because you're forcing me." His smile was barely noticeable.

At the station, a very skinny old man entered the car. He was carrying a paper shopping bag. His chest was so concave, and his back so hunched, that he looked like a question mark without the dot. When the doors closed, he tottered toward a seat.

"I hope I never look like that," whispered Joe.

"You *do* look like that," said Al.

Joe punched him lightly on the arm. As the car lurched, the old man stumbled. Quickly, Al leaned forward to steady him. The train accelerated just as the man began to regain balance; once again he fell back, and once again Al gave him support. Al remembered a children's story he'd recently read to Colleen; it was about a beautiful princess marooned on top of a glass hill. Would-be saviors would mount furious upward charges, only to slide sadly and inexorably back to the bottom.

Al stood up and put his arm around the old man's shoulders. "Damn motormen nowadays," he said. "They don't teach 'em how to drive proper anymore." He steered the man toward a seat.

"I'm going shopping," said the man. His voice was a thin, dry rasp.

65

"I see," said Al.

"I'm seventy-three years of age."

"Nice," said Al. He waited till the old fellow was comfortably settled before returning to Joe and Willie.

"Thank you," the man called after him.

Al waved. "Too bad we can't take him along with us," he said to Joe.

"Too old," said Joe.

"He's younger than you."

"He's too young, then. He can barely move. I think in a strong breeze he'd blow away like so much dust."

"A shame," said Al.

Joe shrugged. "What can you do? I felt like him two days ago."

The train crossed over the Queensboro Bridge on the way to Manhattan. Far below, even in the bright sunshine, the East River was a cloudy blue-brown, gentle swells too muddy to reflect much light. Barges and tugs dotted the length of the waterway; ten thousand toy cars clogged the East River Drive. Ahead, the sky was crowded with the thrusting spires of the city.

"I used to swim in that river," said Willie.

"You did?" said Al.

"Sure. When I was a kid. We lived in Long Island City then, about a block from this bridge. Every summer afternoon you'd have maybe twelve, fifteen kids in the water."

"Bet it was a lot cleaner then," said Joe.

"Oh, it was cleaner," agreed Willie, "but you'd still have the river rats to look out for. Sometimes I'd raise my face from the water, and next to me would be this big, ugly snout—large as cats they were—twitching, covered with fur."

"Scared the hell outa you, I'll bet," said Joe.

"Nah, we was used to it," said Willie. "We'd use the breast stroke, push 'em away with our arms." He paused, remembering, feeling the cool water lapping against his ribs, hearing the shouts of his friends. "The real danger was the current," he said. "It would carry you down toward the harbor, and some days it was pretty strong. Most times, of course, we'd just go with it, swim back to the Queens shore further down or catch the tip of Roosevelt Island. One friend of mine didn't make it though."

"He died?"

"They found his body two days later. My friend, Frankie Calmani. He was eleven years old."

"That was too bad, Willie."

Willie nodded. "It was a long time ago," he said. "A long time ago."

●　●　●　●

They walked south and west, heading generally downtown, their path pretty much aimless, determined mainly by which traffic lights happened to change.

"I hear they may close this place," said Al, when they passed the Radio City Music Hall.

"Geez, I hope not," said Joe. "I used to go here with my kids."

"That's the problem," said Al. "People wanna see adult movies these days. Nobody cares about the children anymore."

"Tell you," said Joe, "the thing my son used to

67

like best was the electric hand driers in the men's room downstairs. He wouldn't even care about the movie. The girls would be watchin' the picture an' he'd say, 'Daddy, take me down,' an' we'd go to that men's room, an' he'd press the buttons on every damn drier in the place. That was his big enjoyment."

They turned down Sixth Avenue, then cut over toward Broadway.

"It's a different era now," said Willie, as they paused under the marquee of the Belasco Theater. "City's dyin'. Middle class is movin' out, government can't pay its bills, Bronx and Brooklyn turnin' to bombed-out graveyards . . . I think the whole thing's gonna collapse on our heads."

"Not my head," said Joe. "I'll be gone."

They reached Broadway. "There!" Willie.

They reached Broadway. "There!" Willie pointed. "There's what's replaced your Radio City and your legitimate stage."

Joe sighted along Willie's shaky index finger. "The Adventures of Marla?" he said.

"Sex shows," affirmed Willie.

They approached the Honeybunch Theater, darting glances at the explicit, lurid photos outside.

"Pornography," said Willie. "It got its place—I ain't no prude—but it makes an area cheap. Brings it down."

"Let's go in," said Al.

"I'll wait outside," said Willie. "I'd be ashamed someone should see me coming from a place like this."

Al laughed. "Come on, Willie, we was just teasing you. We got serious work to do."

"Glad to hear it," said Willie, as they moved on.

"We'll catch this on the way back," said Joe.

At the corner, a crowd was gathered on the sidewalk, blocking pedestrian traffic in both directions. A bearded man in a white sheet stood on a wooden box, gesticulating wildly. The onlookers would occasionally gesture back, occasionally break into laughter.

"They will tumble at your feet!" shouted the orator. "Mark my words: The earth shall tremble at its core and the orifices of sin and defilement will be rent asunder!" He scanned the crowd, his long hair brushing his shoulders, his eyes smoldering.

"Orifices means holes," said Willie to Al. "Don't orifices mean holes? I think he used the wrong word."

"He meant edifices," said a well-dressed man next to Willie.

"See that?" said Joe. "Whyn't you go up an' take over from him, Willie? You could do just as good."

"Maybe I will," said Willie.

"God will cast a pall over the land!" shouted the orator. "He will drive out the purveyors of filth, those who would bestialize the human body, and pitch them into a damnation of eternal, unendurable agony! And thus will those who delight in the carnal pay the price with their own flesh!"

Joe squinted. "On second thought," he said, "I don't believe I will go back to that theater."

"Let's get outa here," said Willie. "This guy's nuts."

They resumed their walk downtown. At Forty-third Street, halfway along the block, they passed a branch of the Chase Manhattan Bank. "For years," said Al, "I thought I had a friend here. Then one day I went to get a loan."

Joe peered inside. "Two guards," he noted. "Both with guns. That would be really tough."

"Forget it," said Al.

They wended their way back toward Broadway, where a veritable sea of people made walking as well as driving almost impossible.

"Jesus," said Joe, "don't nobody work up here? I mean, we're old men, we done our time, but what's everyone else's excuse? The whole world is out on the street."

They heard metallic, syncopated drumbeats. "Somethin's over there causin' the bottleneck," said Joe. The clanky rhythms grew more distinct as they moved on downtown.

"You know," said Willie, "I don't think I been in the city since I stopped driving the cab."

"You ain't missed much," said Joe.

"I have," said Willie. "The changes are slow, but they're there. I see 'em."

A young woman cut ahead of them. She was earing a clinging pink cotton blouse and tight, thin white slacks.

"Look at that," said an awed Willie. "You can see her drawers right through the pants."

"You're supposed to," said Joe. "That's how they design 'em these days."

"Why not just leave off the pants and walk around in the drawers?" said Willie.

Al clicked his tongue. "I'll tell you, it's been a long time for me too. I forgot how many beautiful girls are around here."

"New York's got the best lookin' women in the world," said Willie.

"Lotta good it's gonna do us now," said Joe.

"Yeah," said Al, knowing that this time the teasing was simply the truth. "I suppose. Still, I kinda like to look at 'em."

"Can't arrest you for lookin'," said Joe.

They saw now the source of the hypnotic rhythms: four black treet musicians, a steel band. Silently, Al directed Joe's attention to Willie, who was smiling vacantly and gently bouncing his head in time to the music. A moment later, Al himself was caught-up in the cadences. Gradually, his walk shifted to a kind of home-made-mambo-Jackie Gleason shuffle. Joe began to clap, and several people turned to watch. They were directly in front of the musicians now, and Al began to dance around a slightly embarrassed, but smiling Willie.

"Fred Astaire!" shouted Joe. "Fred and Ginger, right here!"

The crowd joined Joe in his clapping, and this seemed to encourage Al. He two-stepped around Willie with increasing speed. His elbows and forearms flew in all directions. The band, grinning, began to alter their rhythms to conform with his. One of the musicians left his drum and joined Al in his orbit around Willie. After a moment, the three of them joined hands and did a rough approximation of a Zorba-the-Greek dance, with Joe providing the handkerchief. The crowd was now applauding steadily.

Finally, with a grand flourish and drumsticks tossed in the air, the musicians brought their song to a pounding climax. Al raised both hands in the air, then bowed deeply to the appreciative gathering. He, Joe, and Willie all slapped hands with the musicians. Dollar bills littered the street in front of the drums. Amid the crowd, a uniformed policeman applauded along with everyone else.

"Man," said the drummer who'd left his instrument to dance, "you gahs terrific. You the best."

"We enjoyed it," said Willie.

"It was great," puffed Al, still short of breath. Droplets of perspiration beaded his forehead. His cheeks and neck were flushed.

"We best team up," said the drummer. "We get next to a heap o' bread."

"I was thinkin' the same thing," said Al, smiling. "We'll have our agent give your agent a call."

Joe and Willie and Al began to walk again. The crowd had largely dispersed, but several people waved to Al and patted him on the back.

"I was gettin' worried there for a second," said Joe, as they reached Fortieth Street.

"Why's that?" said Willie.

"Well, in the first place, I figured maybe you and Al would take that drummer serious. I mean, with you admirin' them kids in the subway, an' then I could see you were eatin' up the attention of that crowd . . . I figured, these guys ain't cut out for stealin', they oughta be in show biz."

"And what's the second place?" said Al.

"What second place?"

"You said, 'in the first place' about why you was worried. That means there's another reason."

"It does?" said Joe blankly. "I dunno. I forgot."

Al bared his teeth. "Jesus!" he said forcefully.

"I hate that! My mother, God rest her soul, used to do that all the time. Sometimes I'd wait the whole day to see what she had in mind, and she'd never deliver. 'For one thing,' she used to say, and then there'd never be *another* thing. It drove me nuts."

"We can see," said Willie.

"Wait a minute, I just remembered the second place," said Joe.

Al shut his eyes and muttered a mock prayer. "Thank you, O Lord, for grantin' this unworthy soul his poor wish."

"My second worry was that you or Willie or both would suddenly keel over an' drop dead from heart attacks. Then who'd I have to help me pull off the job?"

"Listen," said Willie, "when I was twenty-nine, I went to some doctor on the Grand Concourse. He examines me for a half hour with a stethoscope cold as an ice cube. 'You got six months to live,' he tells me. 'Maybe a year if you're lucky.' I say, 'What's the trouble?' He says, 'Rheumatic heart, young man. When'd you have the fever?' I say, 'What fever? I hardly been sick more'n three days in my life.' He says, 'You got two valves stuck nearly shut. You musta had it.' I tell him I feel fine except for I got this cough. An' I never had no rheumatic fever. He says, 'Yeah, yeah, you had it. A lotta people from the other side had it, they don't even know it.' I explain I was born in the Bronx. He tells me, 'Don't matter anyhow, you'll be dead inside a year.'" Willie smiled. "I guess he was a little off."

Al nodded. "Just goes to prove my point."

"What point?" said Joe. "You didn't make any point."

"I didn't?"

"You ain't said anythin' sensible in a week, if you must know," said Joe.

"Oh, no?" said Al. "Well, here's somethin': To hell with you!"

"Boys, boys!" said Willie. "Fellas, gentlemen, guys . . . relax. Easy. Slow down, and you'll live longer."

"Which brings me back to my original thought," said Al.

"You didn't have no original thought," persisted Joe. "You never have original thoughts."

Al ignored him. "I say: when your time is up, it's up, regardless of anything."

"What the hell's original about that?" muttered Joe. They walked down a street lined with office buildings. "That's the oldest remark in the world, and it's still weak."

"You can live for fifty years," continued Al, "with a heart that flutters like a flag in the breeze, or you can get hit by a car crossin' the street. It's outa our hands."

They were almost back to Sixth Avenue. "You believe in God, Al?" asked Willie suddenly.

"What kinda question is that?" said Al.

"A question."

"That's the kinda thing I'd expect from my nephew."

"But do you?"

Al seemed acutely uncomfortable. "A little."

"What do you mean, a little? Either you do, or you don't."

"I'm afraid not to," said Al. "I mean, I pray to Him an' all, even if I ain't sure He's there, because

74

if I'm wrong"—his eyes twinkled—"there'll be hell to pay."

Joe, whose attention had drifted, pointed at one of the office buildings. "Years ago," he said, "I was walkin', I seen Lloyd Bridges come right outa that buildin'. Remember him, the guy on *Sea Hunt?* Big as life, I spotted him right here."

"My bet is I'll die in my sleep," said Al. "I have that feelin'. If I ain't had no heart attack up to now, I ain't gonna get one. If there is a God, He had plenty of chances to kill me when I was younger, I raised a lotta hell an' drank a lotta booze. So, if He didn't get me then, I figure He'll go easy on me now."

Willie nodded. "How 'bout you, Joe?" he asked. "You a believer?"

"Sure," said Joe easily. "I believe in Lloyd Bridges."

•   •   •   •

The bank was large, its interior tastefully ornate, its architecture marked by sweeping grace. Stepping carefully on the inlaid marble floor, the three men made their way to a long desk on which were stacked rows of white deposit slips and pink-and-orange withdrawal forms. A dozen barred tellers' windows stretched along a counter parallel to one wall. On the opposite side of the room, an elevated, red-carpeted platform set off the management and loan-approval desks.

"Boy," said Joe. "This place is beautiful."

"Looks like a church," whispered Al.

Joe nodded. "Well, whaddaya think?"

"I dunno," said Al.

"Willie?"

"I agree," said Willie. "It's gorgeous."

"I don't mean about that," said Joe. "You know what I mean."

"What're we looking for?" asked Al. "Don't it depend on what we're lookin' for?"

"Yeah, I guess so," said Joe. "I kinda like this one, though. It's real quiet."

"It's so quiet it's holy," said Willie. "Be like stealin' from the Vatican."

"Al?" said Joe.

"I think it'd be all right," said Al.

"You too, Willie?"

Willie shrugged. "It's sure nicer than the one in our neighborhood."

"Well," said Joe. "It looks good to me." He nodded toward a rear corner.

"What?" said Willie. Then he saw. One uniformed guard sitting in a chair, bored expression, heavy-lidded, perhaps in his late fifties.

"I think he'd nod off if you gave him half a chance," said Al.

"We ain't gonna do no better than this," declared Joe. "It's large, it's empty—should we call this the one?"

Al and Willie didn't answer.

"Well?"

"Yeah I guess," said Al finally. "Might as well."

"It's just . . ." said Willie, "you think we ought-ta look at some more?"

"What for?" said Joe. "You think you'll find a bargain somewhere? 'Help yourself' signs over the tills? A bank's a bank."

Willie tightened his lips. "Then this is it."

"Good," said Joe. Out of the corner of his eye,

he saw a woman at one of the desks on the platform hang up a phone and start toward them. "Don't say nothin' stupid now," he said through clenched teeth.

"May I help you?" asked the woman. She was blonde, conservatively dressed. There was slight tone of condescension in her voice.

"Uh . . . not right now," said Joe. "Thank you."

"Are you interested in starting an account?"

"We already—"

"What kind you got?" said Al.

The woman flashed a set of perfect teeth. "Well, basically, there's day-of-deposit, day-of-withdrawal regular savings accounts, and then there are time deposits. If you'd like to step over to my desk, I'd be happy to explain them to you."

Joe leaned forward to poke Al but Al had moved. Joe made believe he was exercising his arm.

"What's the longest time deposit you got?" asked Al.

"Eight years," said the woman.

"That's the one I'm interested in," said Al. "I believe in long-term stability."

Joe rolled his eyes to the ceiling.

"Would you like to come with me and fill out some forms?" asked the woman.

Al looked at Joe, then turned back. "Tell you," he said, "my friend's on his lunch hour now, an' he's got a few things to do. How's about I stop in later, okay?"

"Fine," said the woman. "I'll look forward to it." She returned to her desk.

Outside, Joe walked rapidly, shaking his head. "I believe in long-term stability," he mimicked in a high voice. "She'll give you stability. She'll send you right to jail."

"Ah, I was just havin' me a little fun," said Al. "She was a good-lookin' tomato, even if she was stuck-up . . . an' I like to fool around."

"Just hope she don't remember that when we make our withdrawal," said Joe.

"Come on," said Al. "Where's your sense of humor?"

"I left it outside the bank," said Joe.

At the corner of Bryant Park, they spotted a hot dog vendor and made their way over.

"I love those things," said Al.

"They're the worst food you could eat," said Willie. "At least if you got them from a delicatessen, you'd know you ain't bein' poisoned."

"Yeah, but the taste ain't the same," said Al. "The main flavor comes from the grease they been layin' in, an' the sweat from the guy's filthy hands. You can't get that at no deli." Willie made a face as they reached the stand.

"Three to go," said Joe to the vendor.

The man nodded. "Mustard?"

"Yeah."

"What about them cameras they got there?" asked Al. "I noticed two of'em on the wall."

"That'll be no problem," said Joe. He passed the first hot dog to Al.

"This got onions on it?" Al asked the vendor.

"Right," said the man. "How 'bout the other two? Both with onions?"

"Nah, not on mine," said Willie. "I better not."

"Come on," said Joe. "Live a little. You watch Al. If he don't die from his, then you can eat yours."

"All right," said Willie resignedly. "Onions."

"Everything you got on mine," said Joe to the

vendor. "Ketchup, mustard, axle grease—the works." He saw Willie reach in his pocket and come out with a dollar. "Put that away," he ordered.

"Since when were you such a sport?" said Willie, gingerly nipping off a piece of bun.

Joe received his own hotdog on a paper plate and handed the vendor three bills. "Since today," he said. "These are on me."

Al wiped some mustard off his chin. "This is the best I ever ate," he said.

"Ah, you say that about everything," said Willie. "Last week it was the Alpo, now it's this."

"And next week," Joe chimed in, "it'll be the Chinese food, 'cause that's what we'll be goin' out for every single night."

Willie bit into his hotdog. "You really think this is gonna work, don't you?"

"Dum marr," said Joe, his mouth full, onions hanging from his lips.

"What?"

Joe swallowed. "I say, it don't matter." He held the frank aloft. "I feel like I'm forty again!"

# 6
# Confusing Yesterday With Tomorrow

In the park, the next day, they went over the plans. Joe licked a vanilla ice cream cone as he spoke. "We'll take a gypsy cab there and tell him to wait while we go inside."

"Why a gypsy?" asked Willie.

"Because those guys don't keep a record of where they go or what. We'll give him a good deal and act dopey."

"That won't be hard," said Al.

"He won't figure three old guys'd be up to anything," said Joe. "It won't even dawn on him."

Willie's eyes narrowed. "Yeah, but let's say . . . suppose . . . this guy hears about a bank robbery on the radio. Or reads it in the papers. Three men. Ain't he gonna remember who he was carryin' an' where

81

he let us off? If he goes to the police, an' they start questionin' people in the neighborhood . . ."

"Okay," said Joe. "Good point. To be safe, we take a bus to Corona an' pick up the cab from there. That'll make everything harder to trace."

Al and Willie glanced at each other, obviously impressed. "Boy," said Al. "You must've done *some* stealing during the war. I thought *I* was a thief, but you seem to know all the angles."

"Oh, I never took nothin' big," said Joe. "Only a few tanks."

Al smiled. "And when we get in the bank, what then? Ain't there all kinds of alarms and everything?"

"Yeah, there's alarms," said Al. "The tellers got foot buzzers, and hidden signals that go off when the last dollar bill comes out of the till, and desk alarms, and probably half a dozen things I don't even know about."

"Well, how we gonna beat them?"

"Don't have to," said Joe. "All that stuff don't mean spit. The cops still gotta come, an' that takes time." He swirled his tongue along the side of the ice cream. "The secret is speed."

"In and out."

"Right. But to get speed, the people gotta take you serious. They gotta be scared, gotta figure: Hey, these guys just might be crazy! A stick-up artist I used to know a long time ago told me the most important thing in any robbery is you gotta put fear into everybody right away."

"You put fear into me pretty quick," said Willie.

"All you gotta remember," said Joe, "is that once we get inside there, let me do all the talking. I'll take care of the rest."

82

An old woman from the neighborhood passed their bench. She moved with hunched, painful slowness. The skin on her face was like a crushed paper bag.

"Hello, Mrs. Steinfelt," said Joe.

"Hello," said the old woman as she inched by.

"Hiya," said Al.

"Hi," said Willie.

When she was finally out of earshot, Al said, "I hear she used to be a ravin' beauty."

"That right?" said Joe. "Who told you that?"

"She did," said Al. "I met her once at the laundry. She told me she had four husbands."

"Maybe she'd like you for a fifth," said Willie.

Al made a face. "I'll take some twenty-year-old in one of them miniskirts, if you don't mind."

"An' what would you do with her?" asked Willie.

"Why . . . the same thing I'd do with any other woman." Al smiled.

"I don't think girls that age are interested much in dominoes," said Willie.

"All right, you two," interrupted Joe. "Let's get back to the plannin' here. Let's not get our minds wanderin'. Plenty of time afterwards for wine, women, and song."

"Seems to me," said Al, "the only thing that's left is the timin'. When you think we oughtta do this?"

"When do *you* think we can get the guns?" asked Joe.

"Any time."

"Could you get 'em today, for instance?"

"I guess so," said Al. "Sure."

"Well, if that's the case," said Joe, "then we

might as well go back there tomorrow and make our withdrawal." He stuffed the rest of the cone into his mouth.

"Best to get it over with," agreed Willie. "No sense waitin' till we grow older."

"Al?" said Joe.

"Sounds good to me."

"Okay," said Joe. "Then it's agreed. No more waiting around."

● ● ● ●

The Woolworth store had several counters devoted to masks and disguises.

"The Frankenstein looks good," said Al, trying on an all-rubber model. "It would certainly scare people."

"You wanna scare people, you'd do best leavin' *off* the mask," said Willie.

There were only a few shoppers in the store, mostly mothers and children stocking up on school supplies. Joe examined a gorilla mask that fit over the entire head. "The trouble with all these here is that they're too warm, and you probably can't breathe too good through 'em."

"Probably can't see too good through 'em either," said Al.

Willie had moved around the counter.

"An' look at the prices," said Joe. "You'd have to rob the bank first just to be able to afford these things."

Willie returned wearing a fake plastic nose and a big plastic mustache attached to a pair of eyeglasses. "I think these'd be pretty good. They'd be easy to carry around, easy to take on and off." He puffed on an imaginary cigar. "Say the secret word, and you win a hundred dollars!"

"I think those'd be fine, Willie," said Joe.

Willie removed the glasses. "Oh, you recognized me, huh?"

He led them to the display rack, where they removed two more pair of the comic glasses. Then they trooped up front to the cash register. Joe placed the glasses before the cashier.

"Will that be all, sir?" she said. "Three Groucho disguises?" She flashed a warm smile to Willie, which he found unnerving.

"Boy," he said to Al, "won't the kids love these!"

Al looked puzzled for a second, then said, "Yeah! Oh, sure. Yeah, they will."

"Thank you," said the cashier, as Joe paid the bill. She watched them as they left.

"See?" said Willie.

"See what?" said Joe.

"She's on to us."

"Who? Not the cashier."

"Yes. Her. Exactly," said Willie. "You see her smile? Soon as the news hits the papers about three men in Groucho disguises robbin' a bank—bang! She tells the cops."

"They must sell hundreds of them things every day," said Joe. "And there are thousands of stores, and she don't know us from a hole in the wall. Don't let your imagination run away with you, Willie."

Willie frowned. "Well, we shoulda gone in separately," he said. "Or, better yet, we shoulda each gone into a different store."

Joe nodded. "All right, you got a point."

"But it's too late."

"Yeah," said Joe. "It's too late. We'll know better next time."

●　●　●　●

That afternoon, Al, carrying a folded *News* under his arm, slowly climbed the six steps to the porch of his nephew's house. He peered through the screen door, saw no one inside, and decided to knock. He was not a member of the immediate family; it would not be right simply to walk in. He rapped lightly. "Kathy?"

A man appeared from the kitchen. He was heavy-bearded, short, dressed in a mechanic's uniform. The insignia on his chest read, "A & J Auto." His eyes and arms seemed somehow not to go together. The arms were hairy, knotted with snaky muscles and veins. His eyes were droplets of warm liquid—soft, downcast, retiring. They lit up when he spotted his visitor.

"Pete!" said Al.

"Al! How ya doin'? Come on in." Al's nephew pushed open the door. "I was just on my way out."

Al tried unsuccessfully to conceal his surprise. "What, uh . . . I mean, how come you're home in the middle of the day?"

Pete steered him toward the kitchen, carefully sidestepping a pair of roller skates and an open Candyland game. "Didn't expect to find me at this time, did you?" said Pete.

"Well . . . I'm always glad to see you, you know that," said Al.

They stood for a moment in the living room. "I been taking an early shift over at the station," said Pete. "The boss was real good about lettin' me switch."

"You prefer working in the mornings?"

"Prefer?" Pete wrinkled his nose. "Nah. It ain't a matter of preference. It's a matter of money." He looked over his shoulder toward the kitchen, then lowered his voice. "She, you know . . . I mean, we ain't took a vacation since way before Kevin was born. She don't say nothin', you know, but . . ." His voice trailed off.

"Sure," said Al. "Believe me, I know what you mean."

"Anyway," said Pete, "I picked up a job at night, bartendering up in the Bronx."

"Jeez," said Al, "all the way up in the Bronx, huh? That's rough."

"Yeah . . ." agreed Pete. "Little place in the southeast part. Near Soundview and Westchester Avenues, under the el."

"You work alone?"

Pete grinned. "Well, they got a barmaid to help out, except every hour or so, she's supposed to double as a stripper. That's what they advertise in the window. 'Exotic,' they call her."

"I gather she's not that attractive."

"Well . . . I don't know about attractive," said Pete, "but she has this habit, when she's strippin', of reaching down and taking a little of each customer's drink. She strips on top of the bar, see, and the manager encourages her. Anyway, last week, ten minutes into her little act, she throws up all over the place." He chuckled. "I think a lot of the patrons got turned off. They wanted an exotic dancer, but not *that* exotic."

"It must be rough on you," said Al. "I was a

87

bartender most of my life, so believe me, I know."

Pete shrugged. "Yeah, it's hard . . . but that's the way it goes. The most difficult part is getting my fingernails clean enough after working on them cars all day. That's one thing people don't like to see, a guy servin' drinks with grease on his thumbs."

"You figure you're gonna stay at this place awhile?" asked Al.

Pete nodded. "I have to. You know . . . the kids are growin' up, they need clothes, they eat a lot more. There's not really much choice." His voice softened. "Tell ya, a couple days ago, I got Kathy a pair of earrings—first present since I dunno when. You know, they were little tiny things, circles . . . but she went crazy. She loved them." He shrugged. "That's worth goin' up to the Bronx."

He led Al into the kitchen. Kathy was at the sink, washing dishes. "Kath?" said Pete.

She looked around. "Al! How are you? How you feeling?" She shut off the water, dried her hands with a towel, and came over to kiss Al on the cheek.

"I'm pretty good," said Al. He pointed to the side of her face. "Nice earrings."

She smiled. "Thanks. They were a present from a secret admirer." She paused. "Sit down, I'll give you some coffee."

"Oh no, no," said Al. "No thanks."

"No extra charge."

"No, really," said Al. "I can't stay too long. I was just walking by and thought I'd stop in and say hello."

Pete opened the screen door that led to the tiny backyard. "Kevin!" he called, and waited. There was no answer. "Kevin, what are you doing?"

"Digging," came a small voice.

"Well, get up from there," said Pete. "Where's Colleen?"

"On the side."

"Well, go get her. Uncle Al is here."

Kevin ran to find his sister, and Pete put his hand on Al's shoulder. "Al, I'm sorry, but I gotta get outa here now. You gonna stay for dinner? I'm sure Kath and the kids would love to have you."

"Nah, thanks, not today," said Al. "I gotta go meet Joe and Willie soon."

Pete nodded. "Okay. Up to you. I'll see you then, huh?"

"Yeah, Pete, okay. Don't work too hard, hear?"

Pete kissed Kathy good-bye, then left the room. At the doorway, Al saw Colleen's round face peek quickly in, then move away. He pretended not to notice. Again, the little girl poked her head around till she was just in view, then withdrew. Once more, Al feigned oblivon. The peek-a-boo game continued for another minute until Kevin ran in from behind his sister.

"Hello, Uncle Al!" he said, not stopping in the kitchen, but rushing on into the living room.

Shyly, Colleen pushed open the door. Al knelt and opened his arms wide. "How's my beautiful princess today?"

Colleen giggled, then charged into his loving embrace. "Good," she said.

"Yeah?"

"Uh, huh."

Al smothered her with hugs and kisses. "Were you teasing Uncle Al before?" he asked.

"No."

"But you kept peeking in."

"You saw me?"

89

"Sure. I see everything. How come you didn't just march right over?"

Colleen moved her eyes back and forth. "Mmm . . . I thought you were a monster."

"A monster?"

"Uh, huh.."

"Naw. How could Uncle Al be a monster?"

"Well, I *thought*." She paused. "But then I saw you wasn't."

"Thank you," said Al. "Now, tell me, what were you doing outside."

"Planting," said the little girl.

"Planting what?"

"Seeds. Kevin pulls up the grass, and I plant it so it will grow again."

"I see," said Al. "Very nice."

"Will it be grown yesterday?" asked Colleen.

"She means tomorrow," explained Kathy. "She confuses yesterday and tomorrow."

"Oh . . ." said Al. "Well, I think it'll take longer than tomorrow to grow."

"It won't grow?" said Colleen.

"It'll grow," said Al. "It just takes time."

"Why don't you show Uncle Al the pictures you made?" suggested Kathy.

"I made pictures?" said Colleen.

"You remember. . . . Think."

The little girl smiled sheepishly. "I drew them."

"You did?"

"Uh, huh."

"You think I'd be able to see them?"

"Nuh, uh."

"Colleen!" chided Kathy.

"Okay, you could see them."

"Well, where are they?" asked Al.

"Upstairs," said Colleen. "And I drew them my-self. And Kevin didn't help me."

"I believe you," said Al.

"You want to come with me to see them?"

"Do you want me to?" asked Al.

"Yes."

"Well, okay, then." He turned to Kathy. "See you in a while."

"Follow me," said Colleen. "Make believe I'm a master and you're a dog, and you have to follow me."

"Okay." Al's newspaper was still folded under his arm as they left the kitchen. At the staircase, he called quietly up to the little girl. "You go ahead, sweetheart, and I'll be there in a minute."

"But you're my dog and you have to follow me," said Colleen.

"I will," said Al. "I have to get something . . . a leash. Go ahead, I'll be right up."

Colleen looked at him suspiciously, hesitated, then went on up. Al checked to be sure that Kathy was still in the kitchen before he moved over to open the basement door. His footsteps sounded to him like thunderclaps as he descended the stairs. At the bottom, he spread his newspaper carefully on a ta-ble next to the gun cabinet. Reaching up, his gnarled fingers probed the top surface of the wood and closed finally on the key. In a moment the top drawer was open, and he was peering inside. He removed the pistols one by one, placed them in the paper, and neatly covered them. Fish, he thought. Just like I'm wrapping fish. The second drawer held a confusing mixture of ammunition. *Too much.* Al dumped the contents of the various boxes out on the table, then placed the bullets in his pockets. He closed the drawers and returned the key to its hiding place. At the top of the basement stairs, as he shut off the light, he called softly up to Colleen.

"Uncle Al is coming," he sang. "Here comes Uncle Al."

• • • •

At the stove, Willie scraped the contents of three cans of stew into a pan. Behind him, Joe and Al sat at the kitchen table. The newspaper with the guns lay spread out before them; a pile of bullets, looking like a new kind of cereal, filled a plastic bowl. Joe lifted a pistol and aimed it at the refrigerator.

"All right, you, where's the dough?"

The refrigerator hummed softly.

"Oh, won't talk, huh?" Joe pulled the trigger. "Let's see how tough you are *now*." He pointed the gun at a chair, then the sink, then the stove. "Okay, no nonsense and nobody gets hurt." He paused, nodded, then placed the pistol back on the newspaper. "I shocked them into silence."

"Pete had a million kind of bullets," said Al, who'd been ignoring his friend. "I didn't know which were for which guns, so I took them all. I figured we'd work it out here."

At the stove, Willie stirred the stew "Are we gonna use real bullets? Why do we have to use real ones?"

"Because," said Joe, "if we don't do this thing right, and we get caught, the bleeding hearts in the city will make sure we get put on probation. 'How could you send three sweet old men to prison?'

they'll argue. I'm tellin' you the knee-jerk liberals are everywhere."

"I don't follow . . ." said Willie.

"The cost!" said Joe. "Don't you see? The whole thing'll wind up costin' us a fortune in subway tokens going to see some probation officer. We can't afford it. We gotta make sure they send us to the can."

Willie seemed unconvinced.

"Don't worry about it," soothed Joe. "Like I told these two guys"—he indicated the refrigerator and chair—"if they cooperate, they come out all right."

"What about clothes?" said Willie.

"After the stickup, we get rid of 'em. Just wear something you can throw away."

Al, who'd been studying the bullets, turned around. "You know the best part of this whole thing? We get to wear those disguises. You really picked out good ones, Willie."

"My big contribution," said Willie.

"All right," said Joe. "Here's how it goes. Al, as soon as we get into the bank, I want you to hold your gun on the guard while me and Willie collect the dough."

"What if he ignores me?"

"He won't. Believe me, he won't. If he gives you any trouble, fire a shot in the air. I'm telling you, he'll be scared silly."

"How about other customers?"

"We tell 'em to lie on the floor. Willie and I will watch 'em while we get the money. Any new people come in, anyone come back from the bathroom, just wave your gun, yell they should hit the deck."

"What're you gonna use to collect the dough?" asked Al.

"We'll have 'em fill up that airline bag I got," said Joe. "I figure that oughta hold a nice couple of dollars."

"Especially if they ain't all ones."

"Then we'll get outa there fast," said Joe. "Get back into the gypsy cab."

"And return to Corona . . . or here?"

"Neither," said Joe. "To straight, too easy to trace. We wanna confuse things a little. Instead of taking the cab all the way back, we'll get out and hop into the subway."

"Now you're really talking danger," quipped Willie. "To chance the subway twice in one week— hoo-ha!"

"Once we get past the turnstiles," continued Joe, "we'll transfer the money from the airline bag to a paper bag. That way we dump what somebody maybe spotted or identified, and we ride home on the subway like a bunch of dopey old men. No one's the wiser, and we're scot-free."

Willie looked at Al. "If he wasn't a personal acquaintance, I'd think our roomie was a professional, you know? I'll bet we're livin' with the brains behind the Lufthansa robbery, and don't even know it."

"That was peanuts compared to this," said Joe.

Willie dipped a spoon into the stew, tasted it gingerly. "One last thing . . ." he said.

"Yes?" said Joe.

"Suppose we get shot?"

Joe and Al glanced at each other quickly, amazed that Willie could be so obtuse.

"What's the difference?" said Joe finally.

# 7
# Family Album: Willie

Nineteen oh five, when Willie is born, is a year of the unexpected. A clerk in a Swiss patent office publishes a strange paper; it concludes that the mass of a body increases with velocity, that time can flow at variable rates, that matter and energy are different manifestations of the same thing. The Wright Brothers airplane, first flown two years earlier, has virtually disappeared from the news—*what happened to all the predictions of commercial long-distance flight by 1910?* Instead, a work-oriented, puritan-minded country now seems preoccupied by limericks. Willie's father, a tailor, brings home a new one from one of his customers the night Willie is born:

> "There was an old man of Tarrentum
> Who sat on his false teeth and bent 'em;
> When asked what he'd lost,

And what they had cost,
He replied, "I don't know, I just rent 'em."

Willie's mother doesn't get to hear the rhyme; she dies during childbirth. For the first week of his life, Willie has a fever.

He is a withdrawn, moody child. He is cared for by an aunt in Long Island City during the week and sees his father on the weekends. (Since the tailor shop is in Brighton Beach, at the bottom of Brooklyn, a daily trip is impossible; his father sleeps where he works.) Willie is intelligent, but does not do well in school. Dreamy, his teachers say. Academic subjects—English, math, science—hold no interest for him. He wants to be an artist. His paintings are quite good—watercolors, pastels, line drawings of the two cousins with whom he shares a home. He even captures the resentment on their faces.

He gets a job in the art department at Collier's —layouts, touch-ups, dodging, masking, assorted hackwork of all kinds. The pay is good, and there's a lovely girl, Helen Fitzgerald, in the typing pool who keeps making eyes at him. They get married in 1925, six weeks after Willie's twentieth birthday. They are a loving couple; by 1929 they already have two little boys and a new baby girl. To celebrate the arrival of their sister, Willie takes his sons to see an animated feature creatured by someone named Walt Disney; it involves a cute, crazy mouse, and the kids insist on two complete viewings. A month later, along with a hundred other people, Willie is laid off from his job. He goes work hunting door-to-door, finally lands something in Brooklyn at sixty percent of his former pay.

The country staggers in the throes of the Depression. Willie works twelve hours a day, six days a week, at a dusty textile plant in the Red Hook section. His job involves screen printing on bolts of material. He discovers that if he pulls the cloth real tight as it goes through the machine, he can meet his quota and still have a couple of extra yards left over. Willie is normally no thief, but in 1932, when his children are drinking soup made from potato peelings, he cuts the extra material and sells it. The family lives in upper Manhattan, but he walks to work to save the nickel carfare. *He*, at least, is determined not to be a weekend father. The days, however, seem interminable.

They are not. Two years later, through an uncle of Helen's, he gets a job driving a cab. It is a big improvement over the textile factory, although hardly the occupation the child-artist dreamed of twenty summers earlier. It is to be his life's work for the next thirty-nine years. In 1941, when the second World War breaks out, he is bringing home eighty dollars a week, enough for a three-room apartment in the Bronx, occasional nights at the movies, a Philco console radio. His oldest boy, Bobby, joins the Marines; younger brother Edward, despite the fact that he is only seventeen and has many allergies, manages to get into the Navy. Both boys are assigned to the Pacific. In November, 1942, Bobby returns home on leave. He has survived the battle of the Coral Sea, escaping by lifeboat from the sinking, burning *USS Lexington*. A friend of his has a cousin who has seen Edward. Edward was headed for a pear-shaped island called Guadalcanal.

"I hope he don't suffer from his allergies," Willie tells Helen. "Bobby says the place is all jungle, full of plants."

Edward doesn't suffer. He is shot in the eye while still wading in the water, dead before he hits the beach. The news reaches Willie and his wife a day after Bobby returns to his outfit. Bobby is not as lucky as his brother. He is captured at Bougainville three weeks before Christmas, 1943. The Japanese troops, enraged at their heavy losses, torture and starve their prisoners. Bobby is later found spread-eagled on adjacent palm tree saplings, along with six fellow Marines. Their bodies have been torn apart.

Something goes wrong in Helen's brain. Grief, even vast, prolonged grief, is normal, to be expected. Willie himself mourns for two years. But his wife doesn't come out it. She refuses to eat, to talk, to do housework. She answers questions in one-syllable words. Ten years after her sons' deaths, past Korea and MacArthur-Truman, past the first hydrogen bomb and the Berlin blockade, she still spends her days in a chair, staring straight ahead.

"Doctor Pendergast thinks Mom would be better off in a hospital," says Sandra, Willie's daughter. She has a masters degree in education, has been engaged for six months to a dentist.

"No hospital," declares Willie. "She stays here, at home, with me."

But of course, she is not with him. He is out driving the cab; Sandra cares for her mother during the days. When the Kennedy years come, and Sandra is married, and Helen's condition worsens, Willie has no choice. He commits his wife to the state institution at Central Islip, visits her there every weekend for twelve years, until she passes away.

In 1979, Willie is seventy-four years old. He has a heart condition and is beginning to go bald on top.

He retains a low-key, cynical sense of humor. The occasional watercolors, which he used to do even after he retired, are now a memory. The artist is gone, and his income from Social Security is 237 dollars a month.

# 8

# The Touch of Cold Steel

It is three in the morning. Somewhere on the chilly streets of Astoria a dog barks, and Al looks up. He is in the hallway, having just flushed the toilet in the bathroom. Every night it is the same, urinate three drops, flush, return to his room. He thinks of what a doctor once told him: an old man's prostate is to a young man's prostate as a walnut is to an apple. Maybe I'll get an apple, Al decides now. He heads for the kitchen, passes Willie's room. Willie, Al sees, is sitting by the window, his face bathed in pale blue light. Deep in thought, Willie fails to notice his friend. Al knocks gently on the door.

"Will?"

"Wha?" Startled, Willie spins round.

"What's the matter, Willie?"

For the moment, Willie can't speak. He has been crying an old man's cry, tearless, as if the body had simply run out of juices to expend on emotion. His throat is constricted. "Can't sleep," he whispers finally.

Al moves into the room, puts his arm around Willie's shoulders. "Hey, come on, tell me. *Something's* the matter."

Willie sighs. His voice is barely audible. "I had a dream."

"A dream? About what?"

"I dreamed about Bobby, my older son. How I spanked him once when he was little."

Al nods. "Sometimes your dreams hurt worse than real life. Sometimes—"

"I don't even remember what the whole thing was about," interrupts Willie. "What could it have been? I came home from work, and Helen told me he did something wrong, whatever it was. So I ask him why he did it, and he says he didn't do it. So I smack him on the rear end, and I ask him again. He still says he didn't do it, whatever it was."

"Will—"

"So I smack him again. I was young at the time, and I didn't want him to get the best of me. I was gonna prove something, something about discipline. Can you imagine that?"

"Willie," says Al, "that was a long time ago. A *long* time. I'm sure the boy forgave you. I read somewhere that children really *want* discipline, that they understand it's a form of love."

Willie has turned back to the window. "I kept smacking him across that little rear end of his till he finally says, 'Yeah, yeah,' whatever the hell it was,

102

he did it. Then he ran to his bed and put his face in the pillow and wouldn't look at me."

Al sways back and forth. He doesn't know what to say. The sound of Willie's dry sobs is like a file scraping. "Hey . . . Will . . . come on, Will. Will—"

"We never had any fun after that," chokes Willie. "He only lasted till he was eighteen, that kid. I never got a chance to explain."

Al runs his hand through Willie's thinning hair. He feels the gaunt body quiver, like a dry reed in a wind. "Aw, Willie," he says. "Come on, Willie."

● ● ● ●

Five-thirty a.m. The alarm clock-radio in Joe's room went off softly. Joe reached over to silence it. He sat up, stretched, and climbed off the bed. He felt a surge of rippling energy. Today was special.

He walked out into the hallway. Passing Al's room and then Willie's, he turned on their lights. In the kitchen, he got coffee started then went to brush his teeth. Al had beaten him to it. Still bleary-eyed, he was staring into the bathroom mirror, great globs of mint-green foam obscuring his lips and running down into the hairs on his scrawny chest. A moment later, Willie was peering over Joe's shoulder.

"He's foamin' at the mouth," said Joe. "Must be rabies."

"He uses toothpaste like it's suntan cream," said Willie. He reached forward to tap Al on the shoulder. "You could cover your whole body with what you got on your teeth there."

"Luh muh," said Al, rinsing out.

"No wonder the big tube we bought last week

**103**

is practically gone," said Willie. "Really, you don't have to use that much."

Al put down the plastic cup. "We're gonna be rich in a couple hours. Leave me alone."

Willie peered into the mirror, passed his hand across the stubble on his face. "I dunno if I should shave."

Joe returned to the kitchen.

"You gonna shave?" Willie asked Al.

"I ain't sure," said Al.

"Joe?" yelled Willie.

"What?" said Joe from the kitchen.

"You shaving?"

"Nope," said Joe. "I'm pouring coffee."

Willie looked at the ceiling. "I mean," he said patiently, "are you gonna shave?"

"I'm not," called Joe. "You can if you want to."

Willie shrugged as Al turned to leave. "What the hell for?" he said.

In the kitchen, the three of them sipped their coffee and tried to match up bullets with their pistols.

"Nope," said Joe, attempting to jam a .45 slug into one of the .38 chambers. "No good."

The ammunition was spread all over the table, mingled with the butter, sugar, and toast. "Here," said Al, offering a bullet of smaller diameter. "Try this one."

Joe peered over the top of his reading glasses. "Nah, that'll be too little." He pointed to a bullet that had rolled up to the butter. "Give me that one over here."

Al handed Joe the slug. It fit perfectly in the chamber. "That's it!" said Joe delightedly. "We need more like that."

They sifted through the bullets until Joe had filled up the chamber. As Willie handed across the last slug, it fell into the sugar. Al retrieved it. "Here's some candy-coated persuasion," he said.

With a snap of his wrist, Joe popped the chamber shut. "That's one down," he said

Ten minutes later, three completely loaded revolvers rested near Joe's saucer. "You think maybe we oughtta take some extra bullets along?" asked Al.

"What for?" said Joe.

"Just in case."

"In case of what? We ain't gonna have no shoot-outs." Joe stared at Al for a long moment. "You think we should?"

Al shrugged.

"Ah, what the hell!" said Joe. "Maybe we better take a few. Don't cost nothin'." He slipped some bullets into his pocket.

When breakfast was finished, Joe got his airline bag and placed it on the table next to the three disguises. All the men had on sport jackets, but Al was the only one wearing a black bow tie.

"My" said Willie. "Don't you look snappy."

"He thinks he's goin' to a dance," Joe said.

"I used to wear this when I was bartending," said Al innocently.

Joe handed Groucho glasses to each of them and then indicated the guns. "Take whichever one you like."

"Don't make no difference to me," said Al.

Joe picked up the nearest gun and stuck it in his belt, buttoning his jacket over it. Al did the same. Willie took the last pistol.

"Okay," said Joe. He grabbed the airline bag, spread his legs slightly apart, and made his voice like Edward G. Robinson's. "Let's get goin', you guys."

It was 7:45 in the morning, and the streets were clogged with rush-hour traffic. Joe and Al crossed against the light, Al calmly holding up a hand and bringing two cars to a screeching halt, their drivers cursing. Willie waited for the signal to change before following them. They waited fifteen minutes, then boarded a crowded bus, where they were forced to separate. Al gave his seat in the back to a grateful old woman who seemed far more robust than he did. Joe stood near the front and checked his watch every two minutes, and Willie sat near the door, covering his face with his hands.

"You got a cold?" said an elderly man next to him.

"No," mumbled Willie through his fingers.

"The reason I ask," said the man, "is I see you holding your nose. Truth is, I don't blame you. It stinks in here. If my nose wasn't stuffed, I'd also hold it."

"Allergies," said Willie.

"You're lucky," said the man. "You don't have to inhale the smell. You know what it is? It's the element. The people. The people nowadays stink. Years ago they didn't. Now they do."

Willie nodded, as if contemplating a keen observation. After a while, he noticed the elderly man sniffing, then saw him edging away. Willie stood up as the bus approached the Corona stop. "Tell you the truth," the man called when Willie was halfway to the door, "you stink too."

The three men stood on the corner, watching the bus pull away. Al tapped the front of his jacket to make sure his gun was still well-hidden. Joe looked around. Groups of black men congregated idly on the street. There was a card game in progress on an overturned refrigerator.

"Bad neighborhood," said Al.

"Nah," said Joe. "It's just not white, that's all."

"We gotta watch we don't get mugged."

Joe patted the bulge at his waistline. "Somehow," he said, "I've never felt safer."

They began to walk. "Couldn't we run down the whole thing one more time?" begged Willie.

"Please," said Al. "If we talk it through again, I'm gonna start getting confused. Enough is enough."

"But what if I forget what to do while we're in the bank?" said Willie. "It'll be a disaster."

"Don't you worry about a thing," said Joe. "It's like swimming. It'll come to you."

"Swimming only comes to you if you done it before," said Willie.

"Will, I'll be watching out for you," said Joe. "Believe me. Trust me. Stick by me and stay loose."

"That's what I used to tell my girl friends," said Al. "They didn't believe me either."

Joe spotted a rusty looking cab with half its front bumper missing. "Gypsy," he said. Placing two fingers in his mouth, he produced an ear-splitting whistle. The cab made a sharp U-turn and rolled toward the curb.

"I didn't know you could whistle like that," said Willie, his voice filled with admiration.

"Well, I haven't done it in a while," said Joe, "but as I said, things come to you."

"I used to practice at that for hours," said Willie. "Never could get it, not even once."

The cab came to a halt a yard ahead of them. Joe walked around to the driver's side and leaned in. "How you doin' today?"

The driver was a squat Puerto Rican with bloodshot eyes and yellowish skin. "You chwan a ride?"

"Yeah," said Joe. "Me an' my friends would like to know how much you'd charge to take us to Manhattan and back."

"Manchattan, yes."

"See, one of my friends gotta go to a bank on Fortieth to sign a will."

"A will, yes . . ."

"We'll only be there for about five minutes, the guy's already waiting for us."

The driver stuck his head out of the cab to look at Al and Willie. Al turned sideways. Willie smiled. Three senile old men, he figures, thought Joe.

"Thirty-fi' dollars," said the driver.

Joe clicked his tongue. "Thirty-five," he repeated. "Jesus, that's a lot." He shook his head. "I don't know if we got that much."

The driver narrowed his eyes, hesitating. "Tell ju chwat. Ju look like nice people. I gonna charge ju, mmm, thirty bucks instead. Take fi' dollars off."

Joe smiled and nodded. "It'll be thirty dollars," he told Al and Willie. Not waiting for them to respond, he said, "That's still a lotta money, but okay."

They piled into the cab with surprising vigor.

●　●　●　●

They sat quietly in the back seat, the metal grating of the Queensboro Bridge humming under the taxi's wheels. Willie looked out at the silvery

108

framework of cables and girders, gleaming in the morning sun. "Did I ever tell you?" he said, "I used to swim in the water right under here."

"You told us," said Joe. "You told us."

"Well, here's somethin' you didn't know," Al chimed in. "My father helped build this bridge."

Joe looked at him skeptically.

"Yeah, yeah, he come here from County Cork, right around the Black Hills of Dakota gold rush. He wasn't interested in gold himself—didn't believe there was any, he once told me. He found a job working in the sewers, but it was so damp down there all the time that he started getting the arthritis real bad."

"I hear that's inherited," said Joe.

"Sure it is," said Al. "I got it myself."

"I meant it didn't have nothin' to do with his bein' damp. He woulda got it anyway."

"That, I don't know," said Al, "but, regardless, he got himself work layin' brick on the Brooklyn Bridge. Later on he helped build this here one. He was number two-oh-six in the Bricklayer's Union. Even after he saved up enough to buy the luncheonette in Jersey, he still enjoyed layin' the bricks. He added walls all over the place." Al stared at the bridge's massive towers, following their lines upward to the cerulean sky. "Boy . . ." he whispered, "he's been dead a long time."

Ten minutes later they were creeping crosstown on the congested streets of Manhattan. "So how you guys feelin'?" asked Joe.

"Like I was goin' to my weddin'," said Al.

"Is that good or bad?"

"You're askin' me?" said Al. "I never did make it

109

to my own, you know that. Couple of times I was 'in transit,' as they say, but about halfway there I had a little change of heart."

"And that's how you're feeling now?"

Al smiled. "Don't worry," he said. "You ain't gonna catch me leapin' out of the cab, if that's what you were thinkin'."

"Never crossed my mind," said Joe. He turned to Willie. "And you?"

"I," said Willie slowly, "feel like a million bucks." He was beaming.

Joe raised his eyebrows. "Maybe we should've taken a bigger bag."

The cab eased into Fortieth Street and cruised about halfway down the block before double-parking in front of the bank. The driver swiveled in the seat. "This chwhere jus wanna go, ri'?"

"Right," said Joe. "You wait for us here, okay? We'll be only two minutes."

The driver looked skeptical. "I try," he said, "bu' the cops, they don' like to see ju double park. Sontines they make trouble, chase ju away."

"Tell anyone who gives you trouble that you're waiting for a fare," said Joe. "Tell them we'll be right out." He paused. "Say that if they bother you, you'll take it up with the Taxi Commission."

"Chwa's the Taxi Commission?"

Joe tried to keep the grin off his face, but did not quite succeed. "Look, don't worry about anything," he counseled. "Just wait for us."

"Okay," said the cabbie, "bu' if ju don' see me chwhen ju come out, it means I cruise aroun' the block, an' I be ri' back."

Joe's gaze was unwavering. "Try not to," he said. He turned to Willie and Al. "Ready?"

They nodded.

"Let's go!"

They scrambled out of the cab and headed toward the bank's entrance. There, sheltered by the overhang, they quickly put on the disguises they'd kept in their pockets. Joe and Al, hands on the bulges at the front of their coats, scarcely heard the tiny snap of plastic as they moved toward the revolving door. They were inside the bank before Willie's cry reached them.

"These won't stay on!"

Joe, his hand already gripping his pistol, glanced around. He saw Willie outside on the street, struggling to position his Groucho glasses—one of the temple pieces had broken off.

"Just hold them on!" said Joe urgently. He turned to scan the bank. There were perhaps a dozen customers present in addition to the tellers and executives. The guard had not stirred from his chair in the corner. Calmly, Joe nudged Al in the guard's direction. The man was facing away from them, staring at a woman customer on one of the lines. Joe cleared his throat. When the guard turned, he found himself staring directly into the muzzle of Al's gun.

"What? What're you—"

Al moved the pistol so that the barrel pressed against the man's temple. "Let him feel cold steel," Joe had counseled earlier. "Be it the twentieth century or the tenth, that's always been a sure way to put fear into somebody's heart."

Joe unbuttoned the guard's holster and withdrew the gun. "You so much as blink too fast and, so help me," he said ominously, "my friend here will splatter your brains all over the wall."

Al's eyes widened at Joe's harshness; the threat

111

was more vicious than he'd expected. Still, when the guard's gaze swung slowly toward the gun at his head, his expression all terror, Al managed to keep his own look cool. "Look professional," Joe had said. "Like you don't really mean to kill, but would if you had to."

Joe started toward the counter, gun out ahead of him, airline bag at his side. He saw Willie just inside the door. With his left hand he was pressing the Groucho glasses against his face; his right waved a pistol in the general direction of the guard.

Joe stopped at the rear of one of the lines of customers. "All right," he shouted, "this is a stick-up!"

Several people turned to stare, more out of curiosity or annoyance than fear, while others seemed not to have heard. A few of the tellers looked up.

"It's a stick-up!" repeated Joe. He moved toward one of the cages. All the tellers had now gone rigid. "Touch them buzzers and we start blasting!" he barked.

The customers conversations ceased. The bank was absolutely silent. "I want everyone out here to get down on the floor!" ordered Joe. He swept the gun around expansively.

A few of the customers knelt, but most remained rigidly erect. "I said down!" yelled Joe fiercely. Six women and three men flattened themselves against the floor. Two people didn't. One of these, a black man, squatted on hands and knees; the other, an old woman, simply remained erect. Joe addressed the man. "You hard of hearing?"

The man looked at him sullenly. "Ah down as much as Ah gittin'."

"No, you ain't," said Joe. He aimed the gun carefully at the man's broad face. "Either you kiss that floor or I give you a third eye."

Slowly, his resentment palpable, the man complied. Joe turned to the elderly lady, who was resting heavily on a wooden cane.

"I kent get down, so you vanna shoot, you shoot," she said. "And I'll tell you somethink else, don't think you'll frighten me by givink a third eye. The other two don't work as it is—I got glaucoma on the left side—so for me an extra one vould be a gift."

"All right, just stand still," said Joe. "Now—"

"I'll do what I ken," interrupted the old woman. "I'd like to see you stend still if you had what I got."

Joe knew he'd better ignore her. The slightest display of sympathy or even humanity would result in an hour-long medical report complete with operative history and doctor bills. Instead, he addressed the tellers. "All you back there! Start pushing that money through them windows!"

No one moved. One teller, a young woman, look over at a co-worker, rolled her eyes, and shrugged. Joe became worried; they were not taking him seriously. He whirled at a squeaking sound behind him, saw a young, annoyed-looking executive heading briskly in his direction.

"What is this?" said the man. "I'm the manager here."

"Shut the hell up!" shouted Joe. "Get down on the floor!"

The executive squinted. "Who are you?"

"I said, 'Get down!' "

The man dropped to his knees. "Do you have an account here?" he asked stupidly.

Joe cocked the hammer. "Mister, this is a robbery. One more wise-aleck remark and your head will be a bowling ball."

The executive still seemed skeptical. Possibly he's just reluctant to get his suit dirty, thought Joe. The manager looked up at him sternly. "Are you kidding?" he said. "Is this some kind of joke? Because if it—"

Joe fired at a large wall clock behind the counter. The shot echoed deafeningly around the vaulted interior. Broken glass sprayed the desktop calculators; the minute hand landed intact on somebody's deposit slip. The net effect, however, was salutary; everyone, including Al and Willie, snapped to attention. Quickly, the tellers began to pile money on the counters. The executives and customers—except for the old woman—lay flat on the floor.

"That's better," said Joe. "No nonsense and no one gets hurt." He turned to Willie, saw that he was okay, and turned back. The stacks of bills in front of the windows were growing substantially. "Keep it coming," said Joe. "Keep it coming." He switched to his Edward G. Robinson voice. "And I mean *all* of it. You hear? All of it."

Suddenly, behind him, there was the sound of laughter. He spun, saw two businessmen push through the revolving doors. So absorbed were they in conversation that they seemed oblivious to what was going on.

"Hey!" shouted Willie.

One of the men glanced over at him.

"Yeah, you, fathead!"

Joe was amazed at Willie's aggressiveness. Wil-

114

lie approached the two businessmen and waved his gun in front of their astonished faces. "Both of you! First thing, shut your goddamn mouths. Second, get over there with the others and lie down."

One of the men turned to the other, as if his companion would confirm this was actually happening.

"C'mon," yelled Willie. "Get over there!"

The men walked stiffly to the line of customers and lay down at the end, seemingly determined to maintain their proper place in the queue even under these trying circumstances.

"Yeah," said Willie, still brandishng the pistol theatrically. "That's right. Just lay there and don't get any bright ideas. No one needs a dead hero, understand?"

Joe and Al, who was still covering the guard, exchanged looks of disbelief. Willie sidled over toward Joe. "What?"

"Nothing," said Joe. "Help me fill the bag."

They walked down the counter scooping up the piles of bills. In a moment, the airline bag was overflowing.

"Shoulda brought a laundry sack," muttered Willie.

Joe struggled to close the bag's zipper, finally did so at the expense of a thousand dollars. The tellers, he saw, were staring at him. "All right," he snarled, "I want all of you to lie down also. Let's go! Everyone!"

The tellers dropped to the floor. One young, pretty one smiled at Joe seductively. Her skirt rose along her legs. Joe looked away. "Make it snappy!" he shouted, more to regain his own concentration than to insure compliance.

Al motioned to the guard. "You, too, Pop."

Wordlessly, the guard sank down. For a moment, there was an eerie silence as Al, Joe, and Willie stood among the prone crowd.

"I guess that's it," said Joe quietly. "Let's get out of here."

They were almost to the door when the old woman began to speak. "Listen," she said, "before you go I vanna tell you vun think."

Unaccountably, the men stopped.

"Next time, don't make so much noise," continued the woman. "Everythink else, okay, but that shot was unnecessary. Hurts the ears."

One by one, Joe, Al, and Willie went through the door. Outside, they pocketed the disguises and headed toward the curb. Joe felt an immediate relief; the gypsy cab was still double parked. Holding the airline bag as inconspicuously as possible, he climbed into the back seat. Willie and Al followed. Joe glanced back into the bank as the taxi began to move. He could see no one; everybody was still on the floor. The cab neared the end of the street.

"Any problem?" asked Joe, straining to sound casual.

"Not for me," said the driver.

"Good," said Joe.

"An' chwat about ju?" asked the cabbie. "Did ju sign jour will?"

Joe was surprised the man even remembered. "Yeah," he said. "We're all set. When I die, my entire Social Security check goes to Fluffy."

"Fluffy is jour wife?"

"My cat," said Joe. He leaned forward, smiling,

116

as they came to the corner. "Listen, uh, how about just makin' a right turn here and goin' down to the end of the block, okay? It's a beautiful mornin' out and I think maybe we'll walk around for a while instead of heading straight home." In the rear-view mirror, he could see the driver scowl.

"Chwat abou' the money?"

For just an instant, Joe panicked. Then he understood. "Oh, you mean the thirty bucks?"

"Jes, the thirty bucks."

"Oh, of course, you get it. Sure. A deal's a deal."

The driver relaxed.

"We just figured maybe we'd go to a park," added Joe. "Play checkers or something."

The cab pulled up to the corner of Forty-first Street. A subway entrance was ten feet away. As Al and Willie climbed out, Joe handed the driver three tens and a one.

"Here you go," he said. "Keep the change."

"Thank ju berry much," said the cabbie.

"That's all right."

"Chab a nice day."

"I will," said Joe. "I definitely will."

The three men hurried down the stairs. "Wait a minute, wait!" shouted Willie, trailing behind.

"What's the matter?" Al called back.

Willie pointed to a sign. "This is an IRT. Don't we need a BMT? The other day we took the BMT."

Joe motioned for him to hurry along. After all the years of driving his taxi wherever he wanted to go, Willie was as unfamiliar wth the subway system as a tourist. "We'll change in Queens," said Joe. "Don't worry about it."

At the bottom of the steps, there was a long line

in front of the token booth. Al immediately took a place on the end. "Jesus!" he moaned. "We'll be here for hours."

Joe passed him right by. "No, you won't," he said. "I got tokens already."

Al gleefully followed him to the turnstiles, where Joe fed the tokens into the slots. Out of breath now, the three men walked briskly down to the far end of the platform. Joe looked around. The only person within twenty feet was a drunk propped against one of the peeling walls.

Joe removed a neatly folded brown paper Waldbaum's grocery bag from his jacket. He handed it to Willie. "Hold it open," he ordered.

As Al shielded them with his body, Joe stuffed handfuls of bills from the airline bag into the paper bag. In the distance, there was a faint rumble of heavy machinery. Joe's hands increased their speed.

"Train's comin'," said Al.

The airline bag was still half full.

"Al!" said Joe urgently. "Give me a hand here!"

Al began to assist Joe. There was no concern now about anyone watching; all efforts were concentrated on beating the train. Joe looked around, saw the rapidly approaching headlight pierce the blackness of the tunnel.

"Come on, come on, come on!" he shouted.

The train was at the far end of the platform, and a small mound of bills still remained. Joe reached one more time to snatch up two fistfuls; Al did the same. The gust of wind from the moving cars blew most of the remaining money into the air. The train came to a jerky stop, and the doors slid open. Willie tried to grab some of the loose bills.

"Forget 'em!" shouted Joe.

118

Willie ignored him. Joe handed the now-empty airline bag to Al and pointed to a nearby garbage can. "Throw this in there!"

Al rushed to the can. Joe took the paper bag from Willie, rolled up the top, and plunged toward the train. Halfway down the platform, he could see the conductor peering out to check if all passengers had boarded. He watched Al scramble for the door nearest the garbage can, saw him slip inside the car just as the rubber-lined metal panels slid shut. Suddenly the doors re-opened. A woman thirty feet away had been caught with her handbag outside the train.

"Hold 'em!" yelled Willie. He darted around the platform in a squatting position, grasping at the loose bills.

Joe strained to push back the doors, which once again had started to close. It seemed that Willie had gone completely mad; he was laughing and hopping about crazily.

"Let's go!" Joe shouted.

Willie, breathless, scuttled into the train. His pockets were stuffed with bills. Al had lurched over from the other end of the car, and the three of them quickly found seats as the train sped away from the station.

The subway ride was a time of silence. There was substantial paranoia concerning the other people in the car. There was the fear of assault by the gangly black man gazing at the wall map, by the heavily muscled Latin with the scarred face, by the raucous, radio-carrying group of teen-agers who walked up and down the aisle. But this apprehension was not the usual, low-key, helpless dread of personal assault. This was anxiety born of glorious and magnificent accomplishment. They had done the impossible;

119

they had something worth stealing. And so the focus of their concern was that nothing should spoil the perfection of this most memorable of all mornings.

In this, at least, they were not to be disappointed.

# 9
# Tears' End

They sat at the kitchen table in their undershirts, peering at each other above the stacks of bills. Each of them had a pencil and a sheet of paper. As a group of bills came off the central pile, whoever had taken it would secure it with a rubber band, tally and note the value. Joe was finished first. He stood up, stretched, and walked to the sink to sharpen his pencil.

"How you guys doin'?" he asked.

"Sshh!" said Al, annoyed.

"Sorry, sorry." Joe returned to the table. "Let me know when you're ready," he whispered.

"A minute," said Al. He tallied a final stack of bills, wrote down the figure, looked up. "I'm ready," he announced.

Willie looked up.

"All set?" asked Joe.

"No, I'm not 'all set,'" mimicked Willie. "How the hell can I concentrate with you and him botherin' me every two minutes? What the hell is this, a math contest? A man can't think!"

Joe soothed him. "All right, take your time. No need to rush. Some's a little slower than others, no problem." He winked at Al.

Willie glared at them, but resumed work. Deliberately, enjoying the impatience on Al's face, he counted out the last two piles of bills. He looked up and when he'd jotted down the final number. "Ready," he said calmly.

"I got eleven thousand, five hundred and eighteen dollars," said Joe, writing on the paper bag. "Al?"

"Nine thousand, eight hundred and twenty-one," said Al.

Joe wrote the figure under his own. "Willie?"

"Fourteen thousand, two hundred and sixteen," said Willie, smiling in self-satisfaction. He leaned back in the chair. "Some may be a little slower than others, but some may also *have* a little more than others."

Joe's pencil flitted over the three figures. His lips moved in silent computation. Finally, he gave a low whistle. "Wow," he mumbled.

"What?" said Al.

"Thirty-five thousand, five hundred and fifty-five dollars."

"Holy Mother of Jesus," breathed Willie.

Joe was working on a division problem. "That's . . . eleven thousand, eight hundred and fifty-one dollars apiece," he said after a moment. "Plus change."

"I'll be dipped," marveled Al.

"You can keep the change," said Willie to Joe. "I'm rich. I don't need it."

"I never expected this much," said Joe. "Something, a few grand maybe, but this . . ." He shook his head. "This is great! Damn, it's great!" He clenched his fist and waved it in the air.

"We shoulda hit the safe, too," said Willie reflectively. "We were right there. We shoulda hit the safe."

"Capone, here, ain't satisfied with the haul," said Al. "He thinks you're holdin' out on him, Joe."

Joe narrowed his eyes, assumed the Edward G. Robinson voice. "He'll get everything that's coming to him, you hear? Everything."

"All right," said Willie, "so much for basking in glory. Now what?"

"The first thing we gotta do is get rid of the clothes we wore and get rid of all this cash. We can't keep it around here. If they find out who we are, they'll tear this place to pieces."

"And it would be worth it," said Al.

"What?"

"Just to see the look on Mrs. Flaum's puss. I'd give eleven thousand bucks if she was forced to watch the cops bust up her precious apartment."

"Never mind," said Joe. "It's something we gotta allow for."

"No problem," said Al. "I got a suitcase that I keep at Pete and Kathy's. It has some of my important papers in it, in case something happens."

"What important papers *you* got?" asked Willie. "Collection of bubblegum cartoons? Them puzzles you're always doin' from the *News?*"

"Laugh," said Al. "Go ahead. But when they

find my numbered Swiss account after I kick off, you'll be sorry you wasn't nice to me."

"I won't be sorry," said Willie.

"Does the suitcase have enough room in it?" asked Joe.

Al measured the stacks of bills with his eyes. "Yeah, I think there'd be enough space."

"Does it have a lock on it?"

"Oh, sure. But you know Pete and Kathy. They'd never look into any of my stuff anyway."

"How's that with you, Willie?" asked Joe.

Willie's expression seemed pained. His tongue worked inside his mouth.

"We could find someplace else," offered Joe.

Willie shook his head. At last he said, "Al's suitcase will be fine."

Joe saw that his friend's face was ashen. "Willie . . ."

"Yeah?"

"You feel okay? You look a bit pale."

Willie touched his throat. "Little indigestion," he said. "I think that hotdog I had the other day is finally catching up with me."

"You want something for it?" asked Al. "I got some tablets that—"

"No, no, I'm perfect," said Willie. "You know nothing bad ever happens to the rich."

"Then we'll go ahead and store the dough at Pete's?" said Joe.

"If you guys think it'll be safe over there, it's all right with me," said Willie.

Al stood up. "Well, I oughtta get going then. Pete's been coming home in the afternoons, and I'd like to get the guns back before he gets there."

They began to consolidate the mounds of cash

on the table. Joe noticed that Willie's movements were sluggish and strained, almost as if he were under water.

"I think I'm gonna stop on the way," mused Al, "and pick up some ice cream for the kids. Maybe some toys also. No matter how much they have, it's never enough."

Joe kept staring at Willie. "Will, maybe you oughtta rest a while, huh?"

Willie nodded reluctantly. "Yeah, I suppose," he said. He leaned back heavily. "I'll have to watch what I eat for a while."

● ● ● ●

Pete came home just as Al was leaving. The money, still in the Waldbaum's paper bag, was now resting securely in a locked suitcase in a basement closet.

"Pete," said Al, "how are you?"

"As long as I keep my jobs straight, I'm fine," said Pete. "When a customer says to me, 'Fill 'er up,' I gotta think whether he means J & B or unleaded premium."

"It's tough," said Al. "I know. Bartendin' alone is no picnic, and two jobs. . . . I wish I could help."

Pete reached out to pat his cheek. "Aw, you're a sweetie pie. Thanks, Al."

Al nodded. A slow smile spread across his face. "How do you make a Bronx cocktail?" he asked.

Pete grinned back. "One ounce gin, one ounce vermouth, juice of one-quarter orange. Shake with ice cubes, strain into cocktail glass."

"Son of a gun," said Al. "Not bad. You forgot only two things."

"Two?" said Pete. "Jesus, I thought I had it. Okay, you're the *real* bartender here. Shoot."

"You gotta dust it with grated nutmeg—"

"Ah . . ." scoffed Pete.

"—and it's to be served only when a subway train passes."

"Now *that's* something I didn't know," said Pete. "*That* is learned only after forty years of bartending."

"Try fifty," said Al. He looked at Pete sympathetically. "And hope you never get that much experience."

● ● ● ●

In the park, squealing children ran back and forth under a water sprinkler while the old folks watched from nearby benches.

"Looks good," said Joe. "I feel like going in there and joining 'em."

Willie nodded and patted his face with a handkerchief. He seemed unusually pale. Joe saw his lips working. Next to them on the bench, an old woman was listening to the news on a portable radio.

"You look like you're sick," said Joe. "You feel okay?"

"Fine," said Willie. He belched, and the old woman turned away.

"Should we go get you some Alka-Seltzer or something?"

Willie shook his head. "Nah. The fresh air will take care of it."

Joe stood up. One of the children had fallen while running through the shower. The little boy had landed heavily on his hands and knees; he was

126

now screaming hysterically. Joe walked quickly over and lifted the howling child off the ground. "Shhh," he said softly. "There, there. Easy. You're okay." Tears ran down the boy's cheeks; he was only about four or five years old.

"Show me where it hurts," said Joe.

"Hurts!" wailed the boy.

"Is it your knee?" Joe saw a young woman detach herself from a group of friends and amble in his direction.

"Yes," said the boy bitterly. He held up his tiny hands. They were skinned, but not very badly.

"And your hands too?"

The boy shook his head yes. "I want Mommy!"

"Mommy's coming," said Joe. He was wet from the sprinkler, and the trickle of blood from the boy's knee had made a small stain on his shirt. "Tell you what," continued Joe, "when you get home, ask your Daddy to make you new hands and a new knee."

"Out of wood?" asked the boy.

Joe wiped a tear from the little chin. "Sure . . . tell him to make them out of wood."

The young woman was upon them now. She wore shorts; her hair was in curlers. She was chewing gum. She shook her head in disgust. Joe placed the boy on the ground, and he ran to his mother, hugging her hips and burying his face in her stomach.

"Two seconds!" she said angrily. "You can't play for two seconds without something happening!" She detached him from herself and pulled him roughly along. "Let's go! Come on! Now!" She headed back toward her friends without saying a single word to Joe.

Joe returned to the bench. "You know," he said to Willie, "I don't mind she didn't thank me—that I

127

don't expect—but she didn't even *look* at me. It's like I didn't exist."

The old woman next to Willie turned down her radio. "For her you *don't* exist," she offered. "If she doesn't care about her son, you expect she should notice you?"

"I suppose not," said Joe. He strained to hear. "Excuse me, could you turn up the radio a bit? I'd like to get the weather."

The old woman looked at him skeptically, but nevertheless increased the volume. ". . . partly sunny, but with a chance of afternoon showers," came the announcer's voice. "Precipitation probability is thirty percent today, forty percent tonight and fifty percent tomorrow."

"*This* you're interested in?" said the woman. "After they're finished with all their probabilities, the only thing they've told you is that it may rain. For that, you don't need a radio."

"In this half hour," said the announcer, "new OPEC price hike, Carter to visit Turkey, teamsters demand wage increase, man murdered in Crown Heights, Mets win, Yanks lose, Borg advances. But first—a unique bank robbery in Manhattan."

Joe nudged a beginning-to-doze Willie. "Listen!"

"Not too long after they opened their doors this morning," continued the radio voice, "the Union Marine bank on Fortieth street in Manhattan was taken over by three masked gunmen."

Joe felt his blood racing. "You hear?" he said excitedly. "Gunmen!"

"You're reliving your childhood?" asked the old woman. "You like cops and robbers?"

"Shhh!" said Joe. The woman seemed offended. He'd seen her in the park before—a sour, cynical old crab, he'd always thought—but had never engaged her in conversation. "I think my son has an account there," he whispered urgently. The woman nodded.

"It is believed that the thieves made off with over fifty thousand dollars in cash," said the announcer, "a tidy sum, but hardly unusual in a crime of this type."

"Hardly unusual," echoed Willie, grinning.

"However, what *does* make this robbery different from nearly all others is that the robbers were not the sort of people you might expect."

"I was expecting Billy Carter," said a new voice. Joe turned. It was Al. He slid over on the bench next to Willie. "No problems at all," he said.

"Shh!" ordered Willie.

"Wha? Pete didn't even—"

"Shh! Listen to this!"

"Eyewitnesses at the scene," droned the announcer, "claim that, despite disguises, it was obvious that all three gunmen were well into their seventies."

"Good for them!" said the old woman.

"The Gray Panthers, an organizaton for Senior Citizens' rights, while not claiming any responsibility or prior knowledge of the septuagenarian stickup, do point out that the incident dramatizes what the Panthers call 'the woeful inadequacy' of current government programs that attempt to deal with the elderly. At this time, the police would not discuss the case further, except to state that a full investigation would be launched and that the perpetrators, regardless of age, would be subject to the full penalties of the law." There was a pause. "In a moment, more news . . . but first, *this* about hemorrhoids. Do burning, itching sores make—"

The old woman clicked off the radio. "Last thing I wanna hear is about burning and itching sores," she said. "Bad enough to have 'em, don't need any lectures on 'em." She looked shrewdly at Joe, Willie, and Al. "Nice story about that robbery, huh?"

"Don't sound believable to me," said Joe. I figure the crooks just had *two* disguises, one over the other. The top one covered their faces, the bottom made 'em look like they was old. I mean, I happen to be in the seventies myself, an' you can't convince me someone my age could go and rob no bank."

The woman shrugged and smiled faintly. Could she suspect? wondered Joe. He turned to Al. "Everything go all right?"

"Perfect," said Al. "Pete didn't miss the guns or nothing, and the money is locked up in my suitcase and buried way in the back of one of his closets."

"Well," said Joe, pleased. "Then that's that."

"We're famous," said Willie quietly. "Famous." Beads of perspiration dotted his forehead, and his breathing was rapid and shallow.

"Will?" said Joe. "You don't look so good."

Willie nodded. Rapid swallowing was failing to relieve his nausea. "Still got that stomach trouble, I think."

"You wanna lie down?"

Willie was turning white. "Got some gas pains in my chest," he whispered.

Al stood up. "Try lyin' down," he said. He cast a worried glance at Joe.

"It's nothing," said Willie. "Don't make a big deal. I'm telling you, it'll pass. Don't—" He winced, as a massive pressure seemed to squeeze his ribs up and back into his shoulder blades.

"Will," said Joe, "maybe we should get an ambulance. Just to be on the safe side."

"No," gasped Willie. "No. I'm telling you, it's nothing." But some remote observer inside him was calmly suggesting the opposite. *This is a heart attack*, it noted. *If you don't get help, you'll die right here.* "I'll lay down," he conceded.

Al and Joe stood up. The old woman at the other end of the bench rose and came over. "Here," she said, offering her handbag, "let him rest on this."

Joe slipped it under Willie's head. Willie was grunting and sighing now from the discomfort. "I don't care what he says," barked Joe to Al. "Go call an ambulance."

Al started briskly away, then turned back. "I need some change."

Joe dug three dimes out of his pocket and handed them over. He watched as Al headed out of the park. "All right, he's gonna get some help. Few minutes, everything'll be fine."

Willie's mouth was opening and closing like a fish's. The bloodless flesh of his face was stretched like tissue paper over his cheekbones. "Nnnn," he said. "Nnnn."

"I think we should raise his legs," said the old woman. "I read somewhere, you're supposed to raise the person's legs."

Joe didn't ask her, *What person's legs?* or *Under what conditions?* It was a thing to do when his friend was otherwise totally helpless and seemingly

131

near death. He lifted Willie's feet and hooked them over the back of the bench. "Just hang on a few minutes," he said. "Ambulance is coming."

Willie closed his eyes. "Cold," he whispered. "Cold."

"I'll get you something," said Joe. He ran toward the group of young mothers on the opposite side of the sprinkler. "'Scuse me," he said breathlessly to them. "Would one of you ladies have something I could use to cover my friend?" He pointed back toward the bench. "I think he's havin' a heart attack."

The women, stopped in mid-conversation, just stared.

"He's havin' a heart attack," repeated Joe.

"Oh, my! Here," said a bespectacled brunette finally. She handed a blanket from her baby carriage.

"Take this," said a heavy woman nearby, offering a light jacket.

"Should I call an ambulance?" yelled the brunette as Joe started back.

"Thanks, someone's getting one!" shouted Joe. This will make their day, he reflected. Give them something to talk about for hours. At the bench, he covered Willie's legs with the blanket, laid the jacket over his torso. "Just hold on," he said. "Help'll be here in one minute."

Willie, shuddering, said nothing.

"Funny," commented the old woman. "A hot, sunny day, and he's freezing."

Joe wondered if he should attempt mouth-to-mouth resuscitation, but decided against it. Willie *was* breathing, although laboriously, and chances were he'd do his friend more harm than good. Joe paced nervously back and forth in front of the bench.

A few of the young children began to edge closer, aware that something was wrong. "Move away!" ordered Joe. "Get outta here!" They scattered.

Five minutes later, two of the women detached themselves from the knot of young mothers and came over.

"Is there anything at all we can do to help?" asked the brunette who had offered the blanket.

"I dunno," said Joe. "The ambulance. . . . Maybe, if someone could find a cop . . ."

"I will," said the brunette.

Joe watched the two women retreat to the group, saw the brunette leave her baby carriage and walk rapidly up the path toward the exit. He turned his attention to Willie, who seemed to be squirming, perhaps trying to sit up. "Stay still," ordered Joe. Willie's eyes were open, but the pupils were not focused. "Stay still, or you'll hurt yourself. Keep your feet up!"

Willie's look was pleading, his voice quavering. "I'm scared, Joe. I'm real scared."

Joe stroked his friend's forehead. "I know, I know. But you just rest easy now and things'll be all right. Al's out gettin' an ambulance—you know Al, he probably stopped for a beer first—and soon's they get here, they'll give you somethin' to stop the pain. They got terrific medicines nowadays, terrific . . ."

Willie tugged at his arm. "Sorry," he whispered.

"Aw—"

"Sorry to put you to so much trouble."

"You just rest now, Will."

133

Willie slumped back. Joe looked around desperately, helplessly. Where the hell was the ambulance? It was over a half hour already, why wasn't it here? "This is like a dream," he said to the old lady. "My friend is lyin' here, and everyone is crawling along in a slow motion."

"Terrible," agreed the woman. "A terrible thing to be old and sick."

Five minutes later, Joe felt Willie's gnarled fingers gripping his arm again. Willie was mouthing something, and Joe put his ear close to Willie's lips. "I don't wanna die," he heard. "I'm not ready."

"You won't die," said Joe. "Don't you worry now. I promise, you won't." He stroked Willie's cheek, and looked up at the sky. Damn, he thought. Damn, not now. Not now. His fingers felt wet. He glanced back down. Willie was crying, the tears trickling out from under his closed eyelids. "Ambulance be here in just one minute," said Joe hopelessly.

Presently, the tears stopped.

# 10
# Death of a
# Stickup Man

The total wait for the ambulance was forty-five minutes. When it did appear, it raced through the park, siren wailing, cutting over the grassy areas and finally pulling up next to the bench. A small crowd had now gathered at a discreet distance, and the two white-clad paramedics, accompanied by Al, had to push their way through. One of them immediately opened Willie's shirt and put a stethoscope on his skinny chest. It took less than ten seconds before he said, "We'll need the stretcher." The two men returned to the ambulance.

"What happened?" asked Joe dazedly. He seemed preoccupied with something, distracted.

"I nearly went crazy," said Al. "First I dial nine-one-one, an' I get a busy signal. I wait a minute, try again, same thing. Can you believe it? A busy signal from the emergency number! All right. I look up Elmhurst General Hospital, try them instead. I get through, explain that I think my friend is havin' a heart attack. They say, sorry, we can't do nothin'. You want an ambulance, best bet is to call the fire department. The only way the hospital sends an ambulance is if a doctor requests it, or the police."

"Jesus . . ." said Joe. "Jesus."

"Anyway, I hang up," continued Al. "Then I get an idea. I call back the hospital, get the emergency room, tell 'em my name is Dr. Alan Feeney. I got a patient needs an ambulance immediately, I say. I hear some talkin' in the background, and then another voice comes on and asks if I'm affiliated with the hospital because their records don't list no Dr. Feeney. I tell 'em I'm new, that I signed in last week, and that maybe my name ain't entered in their computers yet."

"That was quick thinkin', Al." The paramedics were returning with the stretcher.

"Didn't do no good," said Al. "Turned out, they don't have no computers. Anyway, after I hung up, I called the local fire department. They got only one cardiac arrest unit, the guys tells me, and that one's out. But they'll put me on the list, and when their truck comes back, I'll be next. I feel like cursin' 'em, but anyway I give 'em all the information they want, and I hang up. I decide to try nine-eleven again. By this time I'm going crazy. I'm so frustrated I just wanna kill myself. I mean, here I am in the center of the biggest city in the world, with my friend maybe dyin'—and I can't get anyone to help me. No one."

The paramedics placed the stretcher at the foot

of the bench. Then the two of them lifted Willie onto it, removed the blanket and jacket, and covered his body with a sheet. "Ready . . . up!" said one. They grabbed the stretcher at the ends and bore it to the ambulance. Joe and Al trailed behind, exhausted, impotent.

"He ain't movin'," said Al quietly, as one of the attendants climbed into the back of the ambulance and helped to hoist the stretcher aboard.

"I know," said Joe. "I know."

"You his family?" asked the older paramedic, indicating Al.

"Friends," said Al.

"We're closer than his family," said Joe. "Can we come along?"

The paramedic nodded. "Ride with me." He extended a hand and helped Al and Joe aboard, while the other attendant raced around to the front.

"Thanks," called Joe to the women who'd supplied the blanket and jacket. He couldn't be sure if they heard. His last sight, as the doors closed behind them, was of the old lady who'd sat with them on the bench. She was trudging slowly up the path, out of the park, her head shaking back and forth. Even at this distance, Joe could see she'd forgotten her handbag.

The ambulance started out, siren wailing. Willie's stretcher was on a raised platform, and the attendant was bending over him, injecting something. The medic was in his late twenties, Joe judged; he had thick, black hair curling down his forehead. After several moments, he turned the knobs on a radio and spoke evenly into a microphone. Joe caught only a few of the words. "Cardiac

. . . pressure, ninety over sixty five . . . vital signs . . . respiration . . . beginning—"

"Is he alive?" asked Al.

The attendant looked up. He seemed not to have heard. His eyes were harried, frantic. "You know, they're supposed to have another goddamned man in here," he said angrily. He made some adjustments on a small metal box, unraveled two long, rubber-clad leads. "I mean, I can't do every goddamn thing myself. Guy's sick, they gotta get a replacement. That's the law, for Chrissake."

He reached over, pulled the sheet to Willie's waist and quickly unbuttoned the old man's outer shirt. He used a razor to cut away the straps of the undershirt. He held the insulated metal prongs at the ends of the leads against Willie's chest. "Do me a favor," he said to Al, indicating the metal box with his chin. "Just hit that button." He paused. "Go on. Don't worry, it don't matter how long you press it, it's all set automatically."

Al hesitated.

"Go on, it's okay."

Al pressed the button. Willie's body flopped and arched like a fish out of water. It seemed his ribs might burst through the skin of his chest. The paramedic immediately placed his stethoscope just below Willie's collarbone. "Okay," he said after a moment. "Okay."

Al looked at Joe apprehensively.

"He gonna make it?" asked Joe.

The paramedic held out his palm, tilted it back and forth. Joe nodded.

The ambulance threaded its way through rush-hour traffic, its siren screaming ineffectually at the slow-to-pull-over cars. It seemed to Joe that they'd been traveling for hours. Willie had electrodes attached to him now; a bluish trace on a tiny portable oscilloscope registered his tenuous, flickering connection with life.

"I had to wait at the phone until they came," said Al. "They needed someone to give 'em directions. That nine-one-one . . . it took so long."

"You done real good," Joe reassured him. "There was nothing more anyone could've accomplished."

At the hospital, there was an impressive display of activity when the ambulance arrived. Two attendants ran out to meet it on the concrete ramp, and quickly hustled the gurney-borne Willie through automatic-opening steel doors. Inside, Joe and Al caught a glimpse of Willie being rolled rapidly through the tiled hallway, oxygen tank and intravenous cart already connected up to him. His face was lost beneath the rubber breathing mask, and the rest of him was covered by a blanket. Already, thought Joe, he looks less than human.

"Are you the people who called the ambulance?" asked a nurse behind the emergency desk.

"Yeah," said Joe.

"We'll need some information."

Joe and Al supplied the statistics as best they could. Willie was seventy-four years old. He lived with them. His only relative was a daughter who resided somewhere in Pennsylvania. They did not know his mother's maiden name. His Medicare card was at home. As far as they were aware, he had no supplementary medical insurance. He had no family physician.

139

"There's a waiting room to your right," said the nurse, when the forms were completed. "We'll let you know how he is when his condition stabilizes."

They thanked her and headed down the corridor.

The waiting room was small—six wooden benches, two vending machines, three ashtrays, a public phone. For the most part, Al and Joe sat in silence, watching the progression of injured people arrive and leave—boys with gashed arms; feverish, screaming infants; moaning old ladies; a man whose bone protruded through the skin of his forearm. It was as if the city were providing a seminar; these are the signs of suffering—blood, bile, sputum, and pus. At 7 p.m., Joe bought a bag of peanuts from one of the machines. He gave half to Al.

"We'll have to bring Willie some pajamas," said Al. "Maybe also a toothbrush and stuff like that."

"We have time," said Joe. "We have time."

A moment later, an intern entered and came over to them. "Joseph Harris?"

"Yes."

"I'm sorry, sir, but your friend died a half hour ago."

Joe nodded slowly and swallowed. He had known, of course, that it would be so, but hearing the pronouncement, hearing somebody *say* it, seemed almost worse than the death itself.

"There was nothin', uh, could be done?" asked Al haltingly. "I mean, I know he was an old man . . . but maybe a transplant, somethin' like that?"

The intern shook his head. "No, it's not really . . . Technically, he was dead on arrival. His heart still showed a faint beat, but his brain activity had completely ceased. We worked on him a while, standard procedure, but apparently he'd died even before he entered the ambulance. Sometimes the resuscitator will get a heart started again, but, uh . . ." He shook his head. "I *am* sorry. He was a close friend, I gather."

"Yes," said Joe.

"Would you like some coffee? I can get you some coffee."

"No, that's all right," said Joe. He turned to Al. "You?"

Al motioned no.

"Uh, as far as the remains . . ." said the intern hesitatingly, "uh, you can just notify the hospital within forty-eight hours as to their disposition. Right now, don't worry about a thing." He paused. "Sorry."

Joe nodded. He waited till the intern had gone, then headed for the phone. "I guess they done what they could," he said.

"I guess so," agreed Al.

Joe put a dime into the slot, dialed, waited, finally heard a voice.

"Bender? This is Joe Harris." The funeral home director was no stranger. When you reached a certain age, people in that line of work became sickeningly familiar.

"How are you, Joe?" said Bender.

"Okay," said Joe. "Listen, uh, I'm down here at Elmhurst General with Al, and, uh . . . Willie just died."

Bender clicked his tongue. "Gee, Joe, sorry to hear it." The ritual sympathy of the professional mourner.

"Yeah, well . . ."

"Was it a long term kind of thing? Something he had?"

"No, just like that," answered Joe. "Doctor said his heart just gave out."

"Shame," said Bender.

"Anyway . . . could you send somebody down here to pick him up?"

"Sure," said Bender. "No problem."

"Me and Al will come over there tonight or tomorrow and settle on all the arrangements with you. And let's do it up nice this time, okay?" He paused. "Fuck the Social Security, we're gonna be taking care of it." He looked at Al, who nodded agreement.

"Look," said Bender, "if you want to work out financing, there's no—"

"This will be cash," snapped Joe. "Dollar bills, American money."

"Please," said Bender, "I didn't mean to insult you. If I did, you have my apologies."

"Yeah, right," said Joe. "Okay, so go ahead with the arrangements." He hung up.

They took a bus back to their apartment, where they sank heavily into kitchen chairs.

"Rough day," said Al.

"Yes," agreed Joe. He forced himself up and over to the refrigerator, where he took out a bottle of cold water. "Want some?" he asked Al.

"Huh? Oh . . . yeah."

Joe poured two glasses, and they both drank. "Maybe Willie didn't amount to much," said Joe, "but he was a helluva stickup man."

Al, too spent and drained to manage even the faintest of smiles, could only nod.

142

• • • •

Later, after Al had called his nephew, the two men went out. Joe was carrying a large paper bag. They walked for several blocks through the residential neighborhood, until they came to a corner where the street light was broken.

"Let me have the noses," said Joe.

Al dug into his pockets and handed him the three Groucho disguises. Joe bent down at the curb and threw them into the sewer. A few feet away, he spotted a garbage can. "Over there," he said.

While Joe held open the paper bag, Al removed the clothing and carefully stuffed it into the pail, being sure to cover each item with its own layer of garbage.

Across the intersection, they paused before another pail. "Boy," said Joe, as he crammed a pair of trousers beneath some watermelon rinds, "this is the longest day I ever lived."

The last item of clothing was a gaberdine jacket. "Dammit," said Joe, "I was so excited this morning, I forgot to wear one that I didn't want to keep." He hesitated, then shoved it savagely into the can. "Aaaahh!" he moaned.

A car honked at them just as they were returning to their building. It coasted to the curb.

"I think it's your nephew," said Joe.

A man got out and came toward them. The darkness still concealed his face.

"Pete?" said Al uncertainly.

"Al, are you okay?" came his nephew's familiar voice.

"Yeah."

The three of them walked into the dim light

143

cast by the building's lobby. "How are you, Joe?" said Pete.

"Well . . . gettin' by," said Joe.

"We felt terrible when we heard about Willie," said Pete, returning his attention to Al.

"Yeah, a shame," said Al.

Kathy got out of the car and came over to join them. "We called you back, Al," she said. "We were worried. We were wondering why no one answered."

"Ah . . . me an' Joe just felt like a walk," said Al. "We didn't wanna stay cooped up."

"Listen," said Pete, "we want you to come over to the house for a couple of days, stay with us. Let us take care of you till this whole thing is over. Whaddaya say?"

Before Al could answer, Joe cut in. "Sounds great to me, Al. You can relax and fool around with the kids. It'll help take your mind off things."

Even with his fatigue-diminished perception, Al could appreciate his friend's gesture. Joe always made things easy, he thought, always smoothed over the rough points in a relationship, even at the cost of personal pain. "You think so, Joe?" he said hoarsely.

"Yeah. Sure."

"Really?"

"Yeah. Come on, stop bein' a baby. Won't hurt you to sleep away from the apartment. Pretend you're going to summer camp."

Al patted Joe's shoulder. "You're a good man," he said. "I'll go up and get some clothes."

"We still have the things you left when you sat for the kids," volunteered Kathy. "They're all cleaned and ironed and waiting for you."

Al hesitated. "Well, maybe I should—"

144

"Come on, Al," urged Pete.

Kathy led Al toward the car, but he stopped at the door and pivoted. "You gonna be all right?" he asked Joe.

Joe feigned irritation. "What, I need you to protect me? What are you talking? Get out of here already. Believe me, at this point, I'd welcome the privacy. Who needs you?"

Al nodded. "See you, Joe," he said. He squeezed awkwardly into the car, with Kathy following.

"Joe," said Pete, "we got plenty of room. You're welcome to join us."

Joe recognized the formal politeness of the offer and was grateful even for its ritual courtesy. "Thanks, Pete, but I'd kinda like to be alone tonight."

"You're sure? We have two kids, you know. An additional playmate would certainly be appreciated."

"No, no, really. You go ahead and take care of your uncle. I'll be fine."

Pete nodded. "Okay. We'll see you, uh—"

"Day after tomorrow," said Joe. "At the funeral."

Pete got into the car. "If you change your mind," he said, leaning out the window, "just give us a call, okay?"

"Right," said Joe.

"You have our number?"

"Yeah, I got it upstairs."

"Good night," said Pete.

Joe saw Al twist in the seat, wave weakly, then slump back. "'Night," said Joe softly. He lingered a moment in the darkness, then headed back toward the building.

The apartment seemed stifling, unnaturally still, soundless. Joe walked slowly to the bedroom and sat down on the edge of his bed. After a while, he removed his shirt and shoes, and watched his toes wiggle through his white socks. Completing the cycle, he thought. An infant could occupy itself for hours, playing with and investigating its extremities. And now, here he was doing the same thing. He stood up, padded over to the closet, and pulled out an old cardboard box.

The old photographs and documents came out in yellowed bunches. A tattered birth certificate: *Joseph Harris, October 14, 1901.* A photo, artificial color added, of himself at age nine. A sepia of young Joe in uniform, World War I. Army discharge papers. A faded plaque, *J. Harris-C. Kaneel, Winners, Dance Marathon, Flatbush,* J. C. Carla, Joe thought. Her name was Carla Kaneel. He could not remember what she looked like. He found another photo, himself at age thirty, hands on hips, hair slicked back, confident to the point of arrogance.

Joe's gaze drifted to the fingers holding the picture, to the dry and wrinkled skin, to the bulbous, arthritic knuckles with their sparse white hairs. He began to tremble, and soon his entire body was shaking. Presently he became aware that he was crying. Then, standing, he saw a dark wet stain spread over his trousers.

"Damn!" he said aloud. "Damn!"

He stuffed the memorabilia back in the carton and waddled down the hall to the bathroom. He removed his trousers and used a towel to clean himself off. Imagine, he thought, crying and pissing in my pants like a three-month-old baby. The cycle was literal, he understood now; the helplessness and

146

dependency were real and inevitable. It would not be much longer before the circle of existence snapped shut forever.

●　●　●　●

Bender was a small man, immaculately dressed and manicured, with a disturbingly soft voice. Joe did not trust people with voices like this; it was unnatural to have them, and people who did were clearly covering something up.

They sat in Bender's tastefully furnished office and went over the arrangements; in a morning phone call, Al had told Joe that anything decided on would be fine with him. Bender consulted a form as he noted the available options.

"As far as the cemetery, we've got space in Woodridge, New Jersey, or Pine Lawn on Long Island. I'm surprised Willie never bought himself a plot."

"Maybe he never expected to die," said Joe.

Bender ignored him. "Unless you want the special section in New Montefiore."

"What's the special section?"

"Concrete vaults only," said Bender. "Concrete is very big this year, a lot of my customers are taking them. The cost is a little steep, I'll grant you, but there's a lot of dignity in stone."

"How much?"

"For the vault? Two thousand. But that includes all cemetery fees and tips for the gravediggers."

"And a regular grave?"

Bender shrugged. "I could get it for you for two-ninety, plus forty dollars to open it up."

"You mean dig it?

147

"Yeah."

"We'll take the two-ninety on Long Island. What's next?"

Bender squinted at the paper. "Let's see . . . Body preparation we went over, moving fees we went over. . . . Flowers. You want flowers in the hearse?"

Joe nodded.

"Okay, that's a hundred. You want a separate limousine for yourself and family? Yes? Okay, that's fifty."

"Fifty bucks just for a car?"

"That includes driver gratuity," Bender explained softly. "Your funeral director is another hundred, plus . . . Let's see—you have your own priest?"

Joe shook his head.

"We'll give you Father Scanlon, a very good man, takes only a fifty-dollar fee. Then, let's see, you'll need use of the chapel, use of the waiting room . . ." Bender's voice trailed off as he checked the form and jotted down more numbers. "Obtaining of the necessary permits is another seventy-five, plus—how many death certificates will you be wanting?"

"Gee, I dunno," said Joe. "Do we need any? I mean, we know he's dead, we don't need proof."

"Well, but there is a death benefit from Social Security, and you'll need a certificate for that. And maybe some other things'll come up, insurance or something—I'll put down three, okay? They're only three-fifty apiece."

"Put 'em down," said Joe, disgusted.

Bender rose, his face flushed with anticipated pleasure. "Well," he said, "I think we're finally ready to select a coffin."

The coffins, on waist-high pedestals, occupied two large rooms. "You know what's coming in this year?" said Bender. "Plastic. Would you believe it? Yeah, yeah, I'm telling you, with the cost of wood, and workmanship what it is—" He stopped before a maroon casket and rapped it with his knuckles. "You hear? Fiberglass. Strong as hell, molded in one piece, this is a real—"

"Forget it," said Joe.

Bender shrugged. "You know, the Jews—it's in the religion—they have to be buried in wood. But the nice part of being Gentile, you got flexibility. This"—he indicated a shiny, light tan box—"is a metal model that's very popular, a very nice buy. Welded seams, sides twenty mils thick, last for centuries."

Joe reached out and touched the coffin; it felt cold to his fingers. "I don't like it."

"All right," said Bender, ushering him into the next room. "I see you have a little better taste, fine. You can't deny a man his due. Personally I happen to agree with you. My father passed away last year, he should rest in peace, I wanted to give him a fitting send-off. I came in here, made a selection. The man didn't have much in his life—I figured, at least let him go out in style. Look around."

There were ten coffins, all wood, all with their covers open. Joe passed slowly by each of them, occasionally running his fingers over a surface to get a feel of the grain. Bender followed, softly quoting prices and supplying information. "Plain pine, six hundred even. Doweled construction, your religious Jews specify this one.

"Walnut, hand rubbed. Nine fifty.

"This one is mahogany, speaks for itself. You

149

see the inside? Velvet. A beautiful, beautiful model. Almost makes you want to jump in and lie down. Fourteen hundred."

"This what you got for your father?" asked Joe.

Bender smiled faintly, led him to an even more luxurious casket. "Dad was buried in cherrywood, ten separate coats of stain. You see that inside? Go ahead, look."

Joe peered in.

"Satin shroud," said Bender. "Best there is."

"How much is this one?" asked Joe.

"This?" Bender grinned patronizingly. "This is two thousand bucks." He paused. "But come, let's go back so you can make your selection."

Now it was Joe's turn to smile. "No need to," he said crisply. "Right here's the one I want."

# 11
# Ten Coats of Stain

It was a bright, chilly autumn day. On the small lawn in front of the funeral home, the morning dew sparkled in the oblique rays of sunlight. Al prodded the grass with his foot, watched the drops of water bead up on his polished shoes. He'd been there for nearly an hour; he was happy now to see Joe coming up the path to join him.

"Are they open yet?" Joe was dressed in a brown suit. His sparse hair was neatly combed.

"Yeah. No one's here yet, though."

"How long you been waitin'?"

"Half hour maybe."

"How come you didn't go in?"

Al shrugged. "Ah, you know, I didn't feel like being there alone."

Joe nodded. "Come on, we might as well see what's doin'."

They headed inside and found Bender in his office. "The coffin's in the chapel," he told them. "It's closed, just like you specified."

"That's the way Willie once told me he wanted it," said Joe. "Can we see it?"

"Sure," said Bender. They walked into the small lobby, then down a carpeted corridor and into the rear of the chapel. Another man joined them, dark-suited, swarthy, curly-haired. "This is Dominick," said Bender. "He'll be your funeral director." Dominick nodded.

Joe and Al fell slightly behind. "I see we got the Mafia," whispered Al.

"Sure," said Joe. "Who do you think owns this type of business? Times get rough, they supply their own customers."

At the front of the chapel was a pulpit and raised platform on which rested the flower-bedecked coffin. The polished wood glowed softly under a row of warm spotlights. Bender's face nearly outshone the casket. "Is it everything I promised?"

"Very nice," said Joe reservedly.

Al echoed the comment.

"A matter of honor," said Bender. "Just because you're returning to dust doesn't mean you have to go back cheap. This will make his people proud. He has family?"

"A daughter," said Joe. "I called her last night. She didn't know if she was coming."

Bender rolled his eyes to the ceiling. "Well, of course," he said, "that's certainly her privilege."

Joe cleared his throat. "Uh, I think it would probably be a good idea, before everyone showed

152

up and all, if we just checked . . . you know . . . the inside. I mean, worse mistakes have been made. . . ."

"Of course, of course," said Bender. "Don't apologize, you're entitled." He looked over at Dominick. "Dom."

The dark-suited man lifted the lid of the coffin. Inside, Joe saw that it was indeed Willie, his face a frozen off-white, his head making a slight depression in the wine-colored satin. Dominick and Bender backed away a discreet distance, as Joe and Al leaned over the coffin.

"Good-bye, Willie," whispered Joe.

"'Bye, Will," said Al. He touched his lips to the dead man's cheek, then drew back at the unexpected coldness.

Joe nodded to Dominick, who came forward and closed the lid.

"The priest'll be here in a moment," said Bender, on the way out of the chapel. "He'll probably want to speak to you a while."

"Fine," said Joe.

Five minutes later, he and Al were in a small room, bare except for a table and chairs, facing a short, fat man with a loud voice. Father Scanlon took notes on a yellow pad, and scanned them frequently through wire-rimmed bifocals.

"Okay, let's see. So . . . He has one daughter, Sandra, and two grandchildren, Edward and Tracy. He—"

"They may not be here," said Joe.

"That's okay," said the priest, checking his notes. "He was a cabdriver for most of his life, was a member of the Masons, mmm . . . lost two sons in the Second World War, sang in the choir at St. Mary's church—"

"That was a long time ago, Father," said Joe. "Very long. As I mentioned, truthfully, Willie . . . uh . . . hadn't really kept up with the religion."

"I understand," said Father Scanlon. "But tell me, was he a charitable man?"

"Oh, he was," said Al. "Most definitely. "You'd never see him pass by a nun without offerin' some contribution."

The priest made a note on his pad. "And did he love his neighbor?"

"He did," said Joe solemnly.

"And was he an honest man?"

Al gave Joe a quick glance. "He was," said Joe, his voice squeaking just a little.

The priest looked up brightly, "Well, then, this should be enough. Do you expect a lot of mourners?"

"Not a lot." Joe rose from his chair. "Uh, Father, one last thing, which Willie had often discussed with me before he died."

"Yes?"

"He hated long speeches, Father. He said, 'At my funeral, I don't want nobody sayin' nothin' that takes more than five minutes.' "

Father Scanlon nodded. In his line of work, flexibility was essential. "I'll do my best," he said courteously. "The wishes of the deceased, of course, come above all else."

Afterward, in the corridor, Al asked Joe when Willie had discussed funeral orations. "Why . . . never," said Joe easily.

"You mean, you made that up?" said Al.

"Sure," said Joe. "I just used my noodle. Willie was a straight, no-nonsense guy. The last thing he'd've wanted was some priest who didn't even

154

know him standin' up and tellin' a lot of lies to people who did." He shrugged. "Stands to reason."

● ● ● ●

Just before midday, they stood in the chapel alone, the thin stream of visitors having temporarily halted. Joe looked at the casket, then back to Al. "Boy, what a day this is," he sighed.

"Be over soon enough," said Al. "And then Willie can rest for a billion years."

"That's a long time to sleep," said Joe.

"Yes it is," agreed Al. "Especially if you don't do no dreamin'."

An hour later, Joe was back in the reception area along with a few of the regulars from the neighborhood.

"I was so shocked when I heard the news," said Mrs. Flaum. She had brought her sister, a thin, scattered woman who went for monthly shock treatments.

"Well, he did go kinda sudden," said Joe.

Mrs. Flaum turned to her sister. "He was such a nice man," she said. "So neat and clean."

"Clean is important," said the sister. "Maybe the most important thing there is."

Joe nodded politely and turned away. Death and hypocrisy went hand in hand, he knew. It was an old story. He wandered back to the rear of the room where Mrs. Spelios was speaking to Karl Krenstmann, an elderly man who owned a house in the neighborhood.

"Soon," Krenstmann was saying, "it's time to move away. "My friends are all leaving, and soon I follow."

Mrs. Spelios seemed puzzled, unsure if the statement was metaphysical—whether "moving away" and "leaving" meant dying—or whether Krenstmann actually intended to sell the house and live somewhere else. She decided on a literal interpretation. "I hear Miami Beach is nice," she said. "Why don't you look into a condominium?"

Krenstmann stared at her through thick glasses. "I'm talking about dying, and you bring up condominiums," he said disdainfully.

Mrs. Spelios shrugged. "So sue me."

Krenstmann looked around. "I'm hungry. My stomach is growling."

"It's a funeral here," she said. "What'd you expect, lobster and filet mignon?"

"Why not?" said Krenstmann. "At the Irish ones you can get something to eat and drink. Those are the affairs I like."

Joe, who'd been listening, cleared his throat. "Hey, Karl," he said, "did you happen to see where Al went?" Al had been missing for over half an hour.

"I think he's next door at Moon's, freshening up a little," said Krenstmann.

"See?" said Joe. "There's a man who takes matters into his own hands."

Joe stepped outside the funeral home and walked the few steps to the bar-and-grill next door. He found Al drinking a beer and absently reading a *Daily News*. Joe sat down on the stool next to him. He and Al were the only customers.

"Nothin' so empty as a bar on a sunny afternoon, huh?" said Joe. He made his voice purposely loud, so that Moon, washing glasses twenty feet away, would hear.

"Only people you get now are the lushes and the deadbeats," said Moon, without glancing up.

"And be grateful for them," said Al. He folded the paper.

"How do you like that?" said Joe, now lowering his voice to a near whisper. "Willie's daughter didn't even show up."

Al drained his glass of beer. "No accountin' for human nature," he said. "One minute it's chasin' starlight, the next it's wallowin' in a cesspool." He held up his glass. "Moon," he called. "Can you fix me up with another?"

Moon waved, *okay.*

"You better take it easy with those," said Joe.

Al pushed the newspaper over and pointed to an article. "Look at this."

Joe began to scan the print, but found himself unable to concentrate. "What's it say?"

"You can't read anymore?"

"Come on, tell me."

Al began to read, picking out certain paragraphs. "Police were besieged by phone calls urging them to abandon investigation of the recent Union Marine Bank robbery in Manhattan. The callers, mostly elderly, argued that the theft, believed committed by three men in their seventies, focussed attention on the problems of the aged, and must've been undertaken only out of desperation. 'To apprehend these men and forcefully bow their heads before the criminal justice system would serve neither society nor humanity,' argued Victor Turpan, leader of Elder Power, an organization of senior citizens."

"The cops'll never listen," said Joe.

Al located another paragraph. "Elsie Soans, a customer in the bank at the time of the robbery,

157

has refused to cooperate with the police, despite the fact that she claims to have gotten a good look at the robbers as they fled the premises. 'Ah seen their faces good when they took off them masks outside,' said the eighty-year-old Ms. Soans, 'but Ah be damned if Ah'm gonna tell no cops about it. An' if they do find those three beauties, they better not bother me, 'cause Ah ain't gonna identify 'em neither. Wha' fo' should I go an' tell on one of mah own?'" Al looked up. "They're making heroes out of us."

Joe nodded. "Funny, it feels like that was fifty years ago."

"It feels like it wasn't us," said Al. "It's like I'm readin' fiction about three strangers."

Moon arrived with the beer. "How 'bout you?" he asked Joe. "Can I get you anything?"

"I don't think so," said Joe. "Somehow, I ain't in a drinkin' mood today."

"Suit youself," said Moon, walking away.

When he was out of earshot, Al said, "Think we'll get caught?"

Joe thought a moment. "Who cares?" he said finally.

When Al and Joe returned to the funeral home, they saw Pete and Kathy signing the visitors' book in the reception area. The kids were with them. Colleen screamed gleefully as she ran to Al, nearly knocking him over when she leaped into his arms.

"How's my little bunny rabbit?" laughed Al, kissing her cheeks.

"Goooood!" squealed Colleen.

"You brought Mommy and Daddy, huh?"

"Yes, and also Kevin."

"Terrific. Aren't you going to say hello to my friend?"

Colleen stared at Joe. "No."

"Why?"

" 'Cause I don't want to."

"Because you forgot his name?"

Colleen frowned. "I know his name."

"You do?" asked Al.

"Uh, huh."

"Well, what is it, sugar plum,"

Colleen moved her eyes back and forth, pausing for dramatic effect. "Joe!"

"Hey!" said Al, applauding. "Right you are. Now, since he knows that you know his name, you don't want to make him feel bad by not saying hello, do you?"

Colleen wrinkled her tiny forehead. "Hello, Joe," she said at last.

Joe smiled. "Hello, sweetheart."

Pete, Kathy, and Kevin gathered around and exchanged greetings with Joe and Al. "Feeling a little better this morning?" Kathy asked Al. "Your friend was quite low last night," she explained to Joe. "I've never seen him so depressed.

"Little better now," said Al. "Takes time."

"How you doing, Joe?" asked Pete.

"Ah, pretty good under the circumstances," said Joe.

"Remember," Pete said, "our offer is still good. Anytime you want to come over for a few days, just say the word."

Joe was somewhat surprised. He'd assumed the courtesy of the previous night was simply good form, and he'd been grateful enough for that. But today's

159

repetition meant they were genuinely inviting him. How extraordinarily kind, he thought. How unusual.

"Thank you," Joe said. "Thank you very much. Right now, I'm fine as is, but I really appreciate your askin', I really do."

"Sure?"

"Yes. Thanks." Joe turned to Al. "Let's escort these good folks to the chapel so they can pay their last respects."

"We'll be with you in a minute," said Kathy. "I'm going to take Colleen to the bathroom first. I see she's crossing her legs already."

"I'll take Kevin," said Pete. "Joe, Al, we'll meet you inside, okay?"

"Fine," said Joe.

At the chapel door, Al paused to say something to the funeral director, while Joe walked inside. He stared at the casket for several seconds before retrieving a bouquet of flowers that had fallen at the foot of the platform. He placed the flowers atop the coffin. "It feels funny to say," he said softly, "but I get the feeling that I'm gonna be joining you real soon, Willie." He looked around quickly then, concerned lest anyone had overheard, but the room was empty. He'd felt compelled to speak as he had, to let Willie know that he would not long be alone. The feeling, only a vague foreboding before his sudden verbalization, had taken shape now. It was as if the cells of his body had somehow banded together to send a chemical message, a telegram delivered by hormones and enzymes: *Soon, we give up.* There was neither fear nor threat implied, only a sense of great fatigue, a desire to end the battle, to rest.

Slowly, Joe walked to the chapel door and leaned out. "Al," he called.

"Yeah," said Al.

"Can I talk to you for a minute?"

Al came inside. "Just goin' over the procedures," he said. "The priest'll be back at seven tonight for the wake service, an' then tomorrow mornin', we'll have the procession to the church startin' at ten-thirty." He noticed Joe seemed in a trance. "What's up?"

Joe looked at him squarely. "Whaddaya say we give twenty-five thousand to Pete?"

"What?"

"You heard me. I'd like to give your nephew twenty-five thousand dollars."

Al was stunned. "You . . . But why?"

Joe shrugged. "That'll still leave us ten thousand, and what the hell were we gonna do with all that money anyway?"

Al puffed out his cheeks and walked around in a small circle. "That . . . well . . . that would be great," he said finally. "But you sure that's okay with you?"

"You know, you must be goin' senile. It was *my* idea, wasn't it?"

Before Al could respond, Kathy, Pete and the children entered the chapel. They filed past the casket, with the adults pausing to kneel and offer a brief, murmured prayer.

Outside, back in the reception room, Al managed to corner Pete, while Joe occupied Kathy.

"Pete, can we talk to you for a minute?"

"Sure," said Pete pleasantly. "Shoot."

"No, no, I mean alone."

161

"Right here's no good?" said Pete.

"Well . . . why don't we go next door?" said Al. "Atmosphere's a little better for what we want to discuss, and in addition there's more privacy."

Pete looked concerned. "Is everything all right? I mean—"

"No, no . . . no problem. Everything's fine."

Back at Moon's, the three of them sat at a table. Kathy had taken the children to a luncheonette for ice cream sodas, and Pete had arranged to meet her there later.

"Want a beer?" Al asked.

"Okay," said Pete.

"Joe?" said Al.

"None for me," said Joe.

"Moon!" called Al. "Could we get two beers here?"

Pete looked at him expectantly. "There was something you wanted to discuss?"

Al nodded. "You know, it was a wonderful thing you done, asking me to stay over. Did me a world of good. The thing is . . . I'm feeling a little better now, and I think I'm gonna go back and stay at my place tonight."

Pete looked both amused and confused. "Okay. Is that what you called me in here for? I mean, you didn't have to be that formal—"

"No, no, there's more to it," said Al. He paused uncertainly. "Look, Pete . . . you can't tell anybody about this, okay?"

Pete grinned.

"Just say okay."

"Okay, okay. Now what's the big secret?"

Al glanced at Joe. "Willie left us a twenty-five-thousand-dollar life insurance policy."

162

Pete whistled. "That's a lotta dough."

"He always said that his daughter had plenty of money already; she's married to some dentist who makes sixty or eighty grand a year. And that's workin' four days a week. Anyway, Willie told us that if he was to go before either of us did, he wanted us to get the twenty-five thousand."

"That was very nice of him," said Pete.

"Now we can't tell nobody about this," continued Al, "because Willie said if his daughter found out she probably would try and sue to get the money."

Pete leaned back in his chair. "Is there a will?"

"Nothing formal," said Al. "Just a sheet of paper, handwritten. But the policy designates us as beneficiaries."

Pete shrugged. "Seems to me she don't have a case."

"Maybe," said Al. He cracked his knuckles. "But regardless, here's the point. I talked it over with Joe, and we decided to give you the twenty-five grand to use as a down payment for your own gas station."

Pete tensed suddenly. "What? What are you—" He stopped as Moon brought over the beers.

"That be all, gents?" asked Moon.

"That's fine for now," said Al.

"I don't understand," said Pete, when Moon had gone.

"Look," said Joe. "We ain't got too much use for twenty-five thousand dollars. I mean, what the hell we gonna do with it, buy a Mercedes? Get us a speedboat? Shack up with some call girls?"

"Wait a minute," said Al, teasing. "Maybe we shouldn't give him the twenty-five—"

163

"The thing me and Al *could* use though, is an extra fifteen bucks a week. Just somethin' to tide us over, you know? Let us take in a movie once in a while, or buy a paper on Sunday. Kinda like an annuity, you might say. Anyway, we figure we give you the twenty-five grand, and in exchange you give us fifteen dollars a week till we die."

"My grandfather lived to a hundred thirty-seven," lied Al.

Joe reached out and took Pete's hand. "What do you say?"

Pete, still stunned, said, "I don't know, I—"

"Just say 'okay'."

Pete nodded. "Okay."

"All right then. It's settled."

"And you better start looking for a station right away," added Al, "because I have a feeling the money'll be coming through pretty soon."

● ● ● ●

There was a light rain on the day of the funeral. Father Scanlon met the tiny procession at the door of Christ the Savior Church, and escorted the casket down the center aisle. There were perhaps twenty people in attendance. After the opening prayers and Bible readings, Father Scanlon delivered a short homily that somehow related Willie's death to salvation and the rebirth of Christ. To Joe, the words and rituals were meaningless. Like Willie, he hadn't been inside a church in twenty years, escept for deaths and marriages. He sat through the eucharist prayer, did not participate in communion, and would probably not even have been aware the Mass was over had he not been called on to help carry the casket back outside to the hearse.

164

In the limousine, on the way to the cemetery, he pointed out at the rain. "Look at that!" he said disgustedly. "Some lousy day to go in the ground, huh?"

"Don't bother Willie none," said Al. "He don't know nothin'. Only people disturbed is the living."

Joe twisted around. "There's hardly any funeral procession. I think there's only one car behind us."

"When you get old, that's the way it is," Al said. "Old people are supposed to die. Chances are, half their friends went before 'em, and their relatives—well, it's like the death of somebody old ain't that much of a tragedy. If a young person goes, then you see a procession stretch back for blocks. But, like I said, doesn't make no difference to the person gettin' buried."

Joe mumbled something, then withdrew into deep thought. As the hearse pulled into the cemetery, he piped up again. "Wasn't much of a speech that priest gave."

Al raised his eyebrows. "Wasn't supposed to be a eulogy. And besides, you yourself told him to keep it short."

"Yeah, yeah, I know," said Joe. "But there's short and sweet, and short and empty. That was just a lot of gabble." He sat back as the cars wound their way through the aisles of the cemetery. Soon they stopped near a low wire fence, and Al and Joe got out. They saw patches of straggling weeds separated by clumps of fuzzy crabgrass. The rain was coming down more heavily now, and Joe turned up the collar of his light jacket.

"I hope the grave ain't too far away," said Al, as they walked round to help unload the coffin.

"Terrible section here," said Joe. "They don't

even take care of it. What kinds crummy cemetery is this?"

Al shook his head. "Joe, you ain't said one kind thing the whole day. Nothing works out perfect, Joe. It don't matter spit whether it's raining, or whether the procession had only one car, or whether there's dandelions growin' on the graves. All that's important is that the people who truly loved Willie are here to say their final good-byes. That's the only thing that counts. Willie's in our memories now, not in this box. The box holds only the shell where he used to live."

Joe nodded grumpily. At the grave, he listened dazedly to the brief committal prayer, then lingered a bit as the small group of friends and neighbors began to depart. The gravediggers were lowering the casket into the rain-softened hole, balancing it on two pieces of heavy white cloth slipped under the ends.

Joe felt Al's hand on his shoulder. "Seems a shame," he said.

"What?" said Al.

"The coffin. Two thousand dollars, used one day, then buried."

"It's not a shame," said Al. "It's a symbol, a sign of our respect."

Joe turned, his eyes tearing. "I wanted him to have *one* nice thing," he said. "One show of class."

"It's a beautiful coffin," said Al.

The gravediggers pulled out the cloth slings. They began to fill back the hole from the nearby mound of dirt. Joe and Al returned to the limousine.

"It had ten separate coats of stain," said Joe. "Imagine, ten separate coats."

# 12
# Only Young Once

They made the limousine driver let them off at the park. The rain had stopped during the ride back, and the sun now peeked through large rents in the cover of gray clouds. Joe and Al crossed slowly to their usual bench and found it unoccupied. Al pulled a newspaper out of a garbage can and used it to wipe the droplets of water from the slats of the bench. Both men sat down heavily.

"Whew!" said Joe. "Am I glad that's over with."

"Me too," said Al. "Well . . . I suppose it had to be, one way or another, sooner or later."

"Ah, but it could've waited," said Joe. "Poor Willie didn't even get to spend any of the dough."

"Yeah, true. But what's there to do with all that money anyways?"

"I dunno." Joe yawned. "You wanna go to the movies?"

"I don't mean what should we do with it right now," Al clarified. "I mean . . . you know . . ."

"No, I don't know," said Joe with surprising vehemence. "What, twenty years from now? When I'm ninety-eight? I don't think they show movies in hell."

Al shrugged.

"Maybe you want to go out to the track and bet a couple of races?" Joe suggested.

"Too tired."

"How about OTB? There's an office two blocks away."

"Ah, that's no fun. If you don't see the actual horses, what's the point?"

"How about bowling?"

Al grinned. He and Joe together could barely lift one ball. "I think I'd rather take a snooze."

"Maybe you oughtta take some vitamins instead," said Joe. "You're always tired lately. Now that we got some money we can afford it."

"They don't really do nothing, do they?"

"I hear they do," said Joe. "Like vitamin C. They say it prevents colds."

"Mrs. Spelios said it gave her diarrhea," said Al.

"Ah, you know her," scoffed Joe. "Ask her about vitamin E."

"What's that do?"

"Supposed to be good for the heart. Also helps your sex life."

"I don't got a sex life," said Al, "so how's it gonna help? So far, these vitamins don't seem worth a damn."

"Vitamin B," said Joe. "That's the one for you. Keeps you alert, stops you from goin' senile."

"Who told you?"

"Old guy in the luncheonette. You know, works sometimes behind the cash register. Seymour, his name is."

"Him? His brain's gone to mush. He's got more loose wheels than the Long Island Rail Road. Don't see where vitamin B done him any good."

"Oh, he knows that," countered Joe. "Said that's because, till now, he ain't been taking *enough.*"

"Ah, that's what they always say."

"Who?"

"Whoever's tryin' somethin' that don't do 'em no good. Pill poppers, joggers, dieters—it's never enough."

Joe grinned. "Listen, I now what we both need, a real lift for the two of us."

"What's that?"

"For the first time in fifteen years, I really crave a vacation." Joe's voice became animated suddenly. "Hey! Why don't we take some of that money and go someplace, someplace nice?"

Al tilted his head. "Like where?"

"Mmm, I dunno. How about Miami?"

"Too hot."

"Canada?"

"Ah, I ain't one for touring. Besides, I read that Quebec is gonna revolt soon. I don't wanna get caught in no fighting."

Joe looked at him accusingly. "You don't wanna do nothing. You ain't interested in the movies, you pooh-pooh every vitamin, the track is too far away, and no vacation place is perfect enough for your

169

tastes. Fine. Then sit here on the bench and watch your fingernails grow."

"And what will you do?"

Joe twisted his neck uncomfortably. "I don't know. Maybe I'll go ta Las Vegas."

"Vegas?"

"Yeah, why the hell not? I've always had to be a two-dollar bettor. Now I can do some real gambling."

Al nodded slowly. "You know, that don't sound too bad."

"Damn right. And you can get some rest besides. *If* you come along, that is. I mean, there's no real touring around there, no sights. You just go, and you gamble, and then come home."

Al was nodding rapidly now. "All right, all right. Good. Real good. So how do we get there?"

Joe grinned. "Well, we can eliminate boats. A car is out, since we don't drive. I'd say the choices are plane, bus, and train."

"Let's take a train," said Al.

"Plane's better," said Joe. "Few hours, you're there. Train takes days. Also, it's tough to sleep on a train."

"Mmm," said Al. "Uh, trouble is, I never been on a plane."

"Me neither," said Joe brightly.

"And you ain't scared?"

Joe grinned. "Can't be worse than pullin' a bank robbery."

Al chuckled. "No, I suppose not."

"Besides, said Joe, "we're only young once."

●　●　●　●

When the fourth knock failed to produce any response, Al pushed open the screen door and walked into the living room..

"Hello-o? Anybody?"

Colleen peeked out from the kitchen.

"Hiya, sugar princess?" said Al.

"Mommy's not here," said Colleen, seeming unsurprised by his presence. She fingered her hair. "I got a haircut."

"You did?"

"Uh, huh. Mommy said my boddles were too long."

"Your what?"

The little girl rolled her eyes in exasperation. *"Boddle* curls. Don't you know what *boddle* curls are?"

"Oh, *bottle* curls . . ."

"That's what I said."

"Ah, I see. Your bottle curls were too long, so Mommy took you for a haircut."

"Mmmm, hmmm."

"Very pretty," said Al. "You look gorgeous. Where is Mommy, by the way?"

"She went next door."

"Oh. Okay."

"She said"—Colleen's face wrinkled with the effort of concentration—"'If anybody calls, I'll be right back.'"

Al walked to the basement door. "That's good. You wait up here, darling. I have to go downstairs and get something."

"I'll come," said Colleen.

"Uh, no, no. You wait. I'll be right up."

"But I wanna come," insisted Colleen.

171

"Well, if you do, who's gonna be up here to watch the house if someone else walks in the door?" Al lingered while Colleen considered this.

"Okay," she said finally. "I'll stay here."

"That's a good girl."

"But you come up soon."

"Right," said Al. He flicked on the light and started down the stairs. In the closet, he wrestled a moment with the suitcase before hauling it out onto the tiled basement floor. He pressed open the snaps, raised the cover, and removed the brown paper bag that held the money. He heard the screen door open upstairs and close. Footsteps drew closer overhead; he could make out Colleen's voice. Then: "Al, is that you?"

It was Kathy. Al took out three large stacks of bills. "Yeah, sweetheart," he called. "Be there in a minute."

He heard her start down the stairs. "Can I help you with something?"

He froze. Two more steps, and she would see him! For just an instant, he felt his throat go dry, his vision blur. Then, recovering, he yelled, "No, no, I'm coming up! I just came to get some of my stuff."

"Anything heavy?"

He jammed wads of bills into his pockets. "Oh, no, just photographs, letters, that sort of thing." His clothes were bulging. He crammed several hundreds into his sleeves, a few more into his shorts, tens into his socks. Then he returned the bag to the suitcase, and the suitcase to the closet. He felt like a scarecrow. I got more stuffing than a sausage, he thought. He walked stiffly up the steps and met Kathy at the top.

"Willie's daughter called," he said. "She invited me and Joe over to her place for a few days."

"And you're going?" Kathy said.

"Yeah, well . . ."

"After she missed the funeral and all?"

Al winced. The logic of lying always required more untruth. Lies multiplied like living things. "She said one of her boys had a hundred-six fever, and that her husband was away at a dental convention. The kid had the measles or somethin', and she was afraid to leave him."

He and Kathy walked into the kitchen. "They have shots now for measles," she said.

"They do?"

She shook her head. "Kid probably never took them. Some people. . . . And imagine, her husband's a dentist."

"Well, anyway, we're goin'," said Al. "It was nice of her to invite us."

"I suppose," said Kathy. "Come, sit down and have some coffee." She walked to the stove to put on a pot of water.

As Al sat down, he heard what sounded like a thunderous crackling of crisp paper. Kathy turned to stare at him.

"These poor bones," said Al, "they just ain't as young as they used to be."

● ● ● ●

Joe had been rushing around the apartment for a half hour, grabbing up underwear, shirts, pants, and toiletries. There was no method to his packing; he simply stuffed everything into an old piece of lug-

173

gage and forced the lid down until it closed. A single suitcase sufficed for both his things and Al's. When he'd finished, and checked that all the burners were out on the stove, and that no water dripped in the sink, and that the windows were shut, he lifted his face to the ceiling and spoke to the air. "Willie, I didn't pack for you, but I hope you're gonna be there with us anyway."

Fifteen minutes later, he met Al in front of the house. "How much money'd ya get?" he asked.

"I took around five thousand," said Al. "You think that'll be enough?" He had purchased two small burlap bags with draw-strings, the sort that are intended for children going off to summer camp. He handed Joe a bag.

"I think we'll be able to squeak by," said Joe. "What's this?"

"Two thousand five hundred. Put it in the suitcase; we'll keep the rest on us."

"You think it's safe?" asked Joe, opening the luggage and jamming in the bag.

"Safer than when it was in that bank." Al stared at the single suitcase. "You got everything in there?"

"Everything."

"You remember my shampoo? And my nail clipper?"

"Everything," repeated Joe, "Includin' your Preparation H. I got us clothes, underwear, toothbrushes, the works." He reached in his pocket. "And I picked this up for you."

Al squinted at the small bottle. "What is it, I ain't got my glasses."

"Vitamins."

"What kind?"

"B-complex plus pantothenic acid."

174

"You hold it for me," Al said warily.

They walked to Ditmars Boulevard and hailed a cab.

"Where to?" asked the driver.

"Airport," said Joe.

"Which one?"

Joe had no idea. He looked to Al, who shrugged. "The big one," said Joe.

"Kennedy?"

"That's it."

The taxi eased out into traffic. A half hour later they were speeding down the Van Wyck Expressway, about to enter the airport. "What terminal?" asked the driver.

"Huh?" said Joe.

"The airline. I gotta know which building you're goin' to."

"I dunno," said Joe. "We don't have our tickets yet."

The cabbie shook his head. "Jesus! . . . Well, where you heading?"

"Las Vegas."

"Vegas. Okay. You could try United, American, or TWA. Pick one."

"TWA," said Joe. It was the airline whose TV commercial he'd seen most recently.

The driver brightened. "Now we're gettin' somewhere."

Five minutes later they pulled up in front of a bustling terminal. Streams of people rushed by in all directions, while cabs, cars, and limousines jockeyed for position. Dozens of blue-uniformed skycaps pushed loaded baggage carts into and out of automatic doors.

"You'll like Vegas," called the cabbie, as Joe re-

175

trieved the suitcase from the trunk. "They got a lotta nice strippers there."

When the taxi pulled away, Al said, "I think I'll try one of those vitamins now."

Joe opened the bottle, handed him an aspirin-sized tablet. "These are chewable, you don't need water."

Al put the pill in his mouth. "When are these supposed to work?"

"I don't know," said Joe. "Give 'em a coupla minutes."

A porter approached them. "Check you in, sir? Take your bag?"

"I don't think so. We're fine as is," Joe said, and Al and he shuffled inside. "You wait here," he said. "I'll get the tickets." Leaving Al sitting on a bench, he strode to a mammoth counter whose sweep was broken by baggage weigh-in stations. "Two to Las Vegas," he told the clerk.

"What flight are you interested in?" asked the clerk.

"Next one out."

"That's Flight nine-one-eight," said the clerk. "Leaves in six minutes. I believe you can still make it, if you hurry."

"Fine," said Joe.

"Just have to confirm there are seats available." The clerk pressed a series of buttons, then stared at a small TV screen in front of him. "No problem. Will this be a check or charge card, sir?"

"Cash," said Joe. "How much?"

The clerk told him, and Joe peeled off the fare from a big roll of bills. "Gate six, upstairs," the clerk called as Joe hastened off.

Al had moved. He was sitting in a special seat

176

that had a coin-operated television attached to the front. "Look at this," he told Joe. "For a quarter you get twenty minutes. Any channel you want. There was a woman here, but I seen her get up and leave, so I figured I'd use the rest of her time."

Joe shook his head and waved the tickets. "This is what you're thinking of? TV? We're on our way to Las Vegas here!"

Al stood up. "That's it? You just buy 'em and that's it?"

"That's it. Come on, we'll drop off the suitcase."

"Amazing," said Al. "You don't need no reservations or nothing like that?"

"Guess not."

"When do we got to be on the plane?"

Joe grinned. "About three minutes."

Al blanched. "You're kidding."

● ● ● ●

Slowly, the 727 taxied to the head of the runway. ". . . flying most of the time at an altitude of thirty-seven thousand feet," the captain was explaining over the PA system. "The weather report ahead is good, and we expect little, if any, turbulence. For your information, it's sunny now in Las Vegas, with a temperature of eighty-four degrees. We request that all passengers remain in their seats and refrain from smoking until the signs are no longer lit. Your flight attendants will do everything in their power to insure your comfort. We'll be back to see you all later; for now, thank you, and we hope you have a pleasant trip." Almost as soon as the voice clicked off, there was a loud roar from the engines. The seats and overhead racks began to vibrate.

"Whoa! What's that rumblin'?" asked Al. He was next to a window.

"You askin' me?" said Joe, trying to keep his teeth from chattering.

"I think the plane's fallin' apart."

They began to move down the runway. "Just close your eyes," said Joe. "Don't worry about it."

"I see the wing," said Al, his voice rising. "It's vibratin' like crazy." They picked up speed. "I think we're shakin' ourselves to pieces!"

The scenery outside began to blur. Runways, towers, other aircraft merged into a strung-out, ghostly continuum. "Oh, my God," said Al softly. "Oh, my God . . . Oh, my God . . ."

The deafening racket lessened, and the immense metal bird lifted gracefully from the ground.

"Oh, shit!" yelled Al.

They rose at a steep angle through the sultry afternoon air. Moments later, they were at a thousand feet, and still climbing.

Al turned to Joe, who hadn't uttered a word. "That was all right," he said.

Joe nodded stiffly. "Didn't bother me at all," he lied.

Al gazed out the window. "Amazin'," he said. "The people look like ants."

"Must be ants you're seein'," said Joe. "We ain't that high yet."

"Only one thing bothers me," said Al.

"What's that?"

"The captain. When he said, 'We'll be back to see you all later.' Now, did he mean the whole crew at the same time?"

178

# 13
# A Run of Luck

It was dusk when they landed at McCarran Airport. By the time they'd gotten a taxi and were heading down the Strip, it was dark. Right from the beginning, Vegas was spectacular. A light show of unexcelled tawdriness, a decadent, rococo mecca of sleaze before you were halfway down its first street.

"Hey, look, there's the Tropicana!" said Al, as they rode by a giant, brightly flashing marquee. "And there's the Aladdin!"

They passed Flamingo Road and turned onto Las Vegas Boulevard. *Wayne Newton,* announced the crimson sign at the Sands. *Vic Damone,* countered a huge, blinking ochre panel at Caesars Palace.

"I heard of these places," said Joe. "Don't Johnny Carson always appear here?"

"Yeah, yeah," said Al. "Look, there's the Rivi-era!"

*Win a Car, 25¢* advertised a sign. *Welcome Teamsters. Free Aspirin. Penny Slots. Craps. Casino. Hugo's Rotisserie.*

"You know where you're goin' yet?" asked the cab driver. At the airport, they'd told him to just drive through town until they made up their minds.

"Maybe you could recommend something?" said Joe. The violent lighting had somehow intimidated him.

"It all depends what you're lookin' for," said the driver. "Different places feature different things. You wanna gamble, there's a hundred joints you could pick. You wanna meet girls, the same. You lookin' just to relax, to swim, to sun, that's a different story. You lookin' for cheap, that's another ballgame. It's all according, see."

"I think we're mainly looking to gamble," said Al. "But the other things are good, too."

The driver seemed to consider. "Well . . . there's a new place on Charleston Boulevard, opened maybe three weeks ago. They probably ain't booked yet. You wanna try there?"

"Sounds good to me," said Al.

The taxi made a right turn and three blocks later stopped at the entrance of the Aces Up hotel. The marquee supported a sign fifty feet high depict-ing a cowboy shooting at an ace-of-spades playing card. The 5000 multicolored incandescent lights that comprised the sign had the eye-numbing intensity of flashbulbs. A constant stream of cars stopped at the curb, and dozens of well-dressed men and glam-orous women swept in and out of the lobby.

**180**

A uniformed man opened the door of Joe and Al's cab. Al grinned at him sheepishly while Joe paid the cabbie. The doorman signaled a bellhop, who removed their suitcase from the trunk. "I'll bring this inside for you, sir," said the boy.

Al smiled amiably. The doorman rocked back and forth on his heels. He cleared his throat. A tip, Al suddenly realized. Of course, that's what he was waiting for. Al reached in his pocket, handed the man a five-dollar bill.

"Thank you, sir!" said the doorman, and he ushered Joe and Al inside.

The lobby was shrouded by velvet carpeting that featured red and yellow aces of the various suits. Just about every available surface was covered; the carpet crept from floor to walls to ceiling. The front desk was carpeted, as were the doors of the men's and ladies' rooms. Carpeting ran up the sides of the gushing, multi-jetted, spotlighted center fountain onto the base of the life-sized Sammy Davis Jr. statue, and into the bank of public telephones. It folded over the garbage pails and standup ashtrays, and enclosed a machine that measured your blood pressure for a quarter.

"Owner must be in the rug business," said Al. Automatically, he was drawn to the only uncarpeted area in the lobby—the glass doors of the casino.

"Go ahead, look around," said Joe. "I'll check us in."

At the desk, he waited several moments before a clerk noticed him. "Do you have a reservation, sir?"

"No, I don't," said Joe.

"Is this a single room you'll be wanting, then?"

181

"Yeah, one room, that's all," said Joe.

"No, I mean, will more than one person be occupying the room?"

"Yeah," said Joe. "Sure. Me and my friend."

The clerk consulted a ledger. "Well, we have a double room available in the Hearts wing for the next three nights. Will that be okay?"

"Fine," said Joe. He signed in.

"And will this be cash or charge?" asked the clerk.

"Cash."

"We'll need one day's deposit, sir, if you don't mind. Just step to the cashier's window."

Joe paid the deposit, then returned to Al, who was still peering through the casino doors. A panorama of roulette wheels, blackjack tables, craps tables, miniskirted waitresses, women dealers, and ace-shaped chandeliers spread out before them.

"Just like in the movies, eh?" said Joe.

"Last time I seen so many people in one place was the Forty-Second-Street Cafeteria," said Al. "And the women! They're all fallin' out of their dresses."

"Come on," said Joe, "Let's go upstairs and check into the room."

"I think I'll stay here," said Al.

"Never mind." Joe signaled the bellhop, who was waiting with their suitcase. "You were feeling tired earlier?"

"Yeah. So?"

"So now's the time to take a nap."

"And what're you doing?"

Joe shrugged. "Oh, I guess I'll go up and change my clothes."

"And then?"

"And then, maybe, come down and try my luck," added Joe, grinning.

Al laughed. "Forget that nap nonsense. I think them vitamins just hit me."

In the room, they changed quickly into sport jackets and slacks. Al put on his bow tie, then wandered into the bathroom while Joe was tying his shoelaces.

"Hey, they got two different lights in here," called Al. "One's regular, one's pink."

"I think the pink one's supposed to help you dry off after a shower," said Joe.

Al emerged shaking his head. "Next thing, they'll have a lamp in the toilet so's to make things interesting when you pee."

Five minutes later they were standing in the casino. Surrounding them was a tableau of spinning roulette wheels, chain-smoking women who held stacks of blue and white chips, expertly manicured blackjack dealers, squint-eyed pit bosses and slotmen, convention members with pinned-on name tags, hyped-up newlyweds on honeymoons, matrons on tour with B'nai B'rith, vacationing electrical engineers with "systems," shills paid by the house to sit and gamble, floorwalkers and shift bosses, narrow-tied craps stickmen.

"If the cops just came in and arrested everyone," said Al, "I'll bet they wouldn't go far wrong. This here is the most wicked looking place since Sodom and Gomorrha."

"Oh, yeah?" said Joe. "Did you see that, too? Besides, you ain't even been next door yet." He pointed to an ace-shaped exit. "I hear they got over a thousand slot machines in there."

Al grinned. "You ready to play?"

Joe nodded. "Let's knock 'em dead."

They began with roulette, betting various combinations of numbers and colors, and became bored after losing a hundred dollars. "This here is basically for women and children," said Joe as they left the table. "This, keno, and the slots keeps 'em busy while the men do the real gamblin'."

"What's the real gambling?" said Al.

Joe sat down at a blackjack table. "Right here'll get us a good start."

A grim-faced dealer peeled out cards. The table had a minimum bet of one dollar, a maximum of five hundred dollars. There were positions for six players, although two of the chairs were unoccupied. "I used to play this as a kid," said Al, "but I forgot how it goes."

A sign lettered on the table said: *Dealer must stand on 17 and must draw to 16*. A player on the extreme right said, "Double down." Another man called, "Stand," and then it was Joe's turn. "Hit me," he said, and crooked a finger. He had bet three hundred dollars. His hole card was a seven, his face-up card an eight. Now he glared disgustedly at the card he'd been dealt, a nine. He was over twenty-one. Busted. He stood up. "Enough of this," he said. "Time to move to a man's game."

"I thought you said *this* was a man's game," challenged Al.

"You listen to everything I tell you?" said Joe.

They edged over to one of the large craps tables. Eight bettors and five dealers, casino employees, stood around it. Al watched as the bettors placed chips in various boxes marked on the green felt surface. A man chewing on a cigar threw two dice up against the padded end of the table.

"EEE-eight!" shouted one of the casino men, holding the dice trapped with a curved stick. "Pay the line!"

Two other dealers collected and disbursed varying quantities of chips. When the new bets were placed, the stickman released the dice to the cigar-chewer, who rolled them again.

"Nine!" yelled the stickman. "The point is nine."

More bets were placed. Again, the dice were thrown.

"Yo-leven!"

Al turned to Joe. "You follow this?"

"It looks the same like we used to play during the first World War. I learned it in France." Joe chuckled. "We played it in the halls in the hospital."

"F-i-i-i-i-ive!" called the stickman.

"I'll explain it to you," Joe told Al. "Basically, your first roll is called a come-out. You roll a seven or eleven on the come-out, you win immediately. You roll a two, three, or twelve, you lose. If you roll somethin' else, that's called your point. The whole idea then is to shoot your point again *before* you roll a seven. Do that, and you win. Roll a seven, you lose."

"That's all there is to it?" said Al. "And all these years I never gambled because I always figured the rules was too crazy."

Joe's eyes sparkled. "It ain't the rules that kill you," he said, "it's the bettin'." He reached into his pocket and withdrew a thick wad of bills. To one of the dealers, he said, "We'd like to get a thousand dollars worth of chips, please."

The dealer stacked the bills neatly and crisply, then handed them to the boxman, who quickly examined and counted them. The boxman nodded, and the dealer shoved four stacks of chips over to Joe.

"Sevvv-en!" chanted the stickman, at the next throw of the dice.

"He loses, right?" said Al, as losing bets were cleared off the table.

"Hey, I got it!" He looked over at the cigar-chewer, who glared at him. When he returned his gaze sheepishly to the table, he saw that the stickman had shoved five dice in front of Joe's chips.

"Is it your turn?" Al asked.

"No, yours," said Joe, smiling.

"What?"

"Go. Play."

"What do I do?"

"Take two of the dice and throw 'em."

Al meekly reached for two dice, and the stickman swept the others away.

"You gonna bet?" Al asked Joe.

Joe nodded. He moved two fifty-dollar chips onto a space on the felt marked *Pass Line.* "A hundred on the line," he said. "See Al, I'm bettin' you're gonna win. Throw 'em nice, now."

Al threw the dice in the air, a hesitant, feeble toss that carried only halfway down the table.

"Fi-ive!" called the stickman. "The point is five."

"Now you gotta get a five before you get a seven," said Joe. He turned to the dealer. "You give odds on the five?"

"Three to two, sir."

"All right," said Joe. "I'd like to put another two hundred on the five. Where do I do that?"

The dealer pointed to a space directly behind Joe's original bet. "One hundred only, sir. Can't bet more than your initial wager when you take the odds."

Joe placed two more fifty-dollar chips where the man had indicated, and the stickman swept the dice back to Al. "Sir, could you throw them so that they bounce off the wall at the other end of the table?"

"Helps stop cheatin'," whispered Joe.

"I'll try," said Al stiffly. He smiled nervously at the dealer. "It's still my turn?"

The dealer nodded, and Al threw the dice. They smacked into the end wall of the table and caromed crazily back to the center.

"Ten! Easy ten." The stickman shoved the dice back to Al.

"Again?" said Al, looking at Joe, who nodded.

Another toss.

"EEE-eight!"

Once more, Al threw.

"Fi-i-ive!" intoned the stickman. "Pay the line."

Joe clapped Al on the shoulder. "Hey! Attaboy!"

"What happened? We win?"

"That's right."

The dealer placed a small stack of new chips in front of them, and the stickman returned the dice to Al. "You're still up, sir."

Joe placed three hundred-dollar chips on the *Pass Line* space. "This says my friend is gonna throw 'em right."

Al smiled and threw.

"Sevv-en! Pay the line!"

"Al!" shouted Joe. "You're doing all right." He added the three new hundred-dollar chips the dealer gave him to his stack.

"We won again, huh?"

"You gettin' bored?"

Al smiled. "This is easy."

"Another three hundred on the line for my friend," said Joe, shoving forward the chips. Al threw the dice.

"Sevv-en! Pay the line!"

Joe turned slowly to look at Al, and a woman, showing exceptional cleavage smiled at him from across the table. When Joe said, "Five hundred on lucky fingers over here," she matched his chips at the *Pass Line*.

Al flung the dice with exaggerated carelessness.

"Yo-leven!" called the stickman.

"Uh-oh," said Al. He was surprised when the dealer piled five new hundred-dollar chips in front of him. "You mean that was good?"

"Sure," said Joe. "Remember what I told you? Seven or eleven wins on the first roll."

"But I been throwin' for a long time."

"No, no. When you win, the next toss is considered like you're goin' the first time again."

"I see, I see," said Al.

"You don't have to see nothin'," said Joe. "Just keep burnin' in them dice." He moved a thousand dollars worth of chips onto the *Pass Line*.

"Five hundred dollar limit, sir," said the dealer.

"You gotta be kidding," said Joe. "What is this, a kid's game?"

"I'm sorry, sir," said the dealer. "That's the limit for this table. You can bet on as many different numbers as you like, but only up to five hundred dollars on each."

There was something about the man's voice, his tone, that sent a subliminal tingling down Joe's spine.

Impulsively, he snatched back his thousand dollars, and bet instead a single twenty-five dollar chip. "Okay, pal. This says my friend hits it again. Go ahead, Al."

Al grew tense. "Something wrong?"

"No, no. Not at all."

"But how come—"

"Just roll."

Al threw the dice. The upturned faces showed a one and a two. "Craps!" called the stickman.

The dealers cleared off the losing bets. The woman with the cleavage, who had withdrawn her wager when Joe had reduced his, called out, "Come on, honey!"

"I'm feeling lucky," said Joe. "Let's go for all the numbers."

"What's that?" asked Al.

"I'll show you," said Joe. He leaned forward and began depositing stacks of chips on boxes marked with individual digits. "Five hundred on the four, five hundred on the five, five hundred on the six, the eight, the nine, and . . . five hundred on the ten." He sat back.

Many of the other bettors were now staring at Joe and Al. The cleavage woman bet fifty-dollar chips at all the points Joe had covered. A tall man with a Stetson hat did the same with hundred dollar chips.

"What do I gotta get?" asked Al.

"All you have to do is roll one of these numbers before you throw a seven," said Joe. "Simple."

"Are you ready, gentlemen?" asked the stickman.

"We sure are," said Joe.

"My friend thinks we are," said Al.

"C'mon," said Joe. "Show the man some numbers."

Al took the dice and bounced them easily off the end wall of the table. He'd finally gotten the hang of throwing; he was beginning to feel a kind of subconscious control, a sense of being in charge. It was a potentially dangerous sensation, he knew, and yet it refused to evaporate.

"Six," called the stickman. "The point is six."

"Is that good?" asked Al.

"First roll don't count when you go for numbers," said Joe.

The woman with the cleavage shouted, "Do it for me, sweetheart!"

"Do it for her," said Joe, as the stickman handed the dice back to Al.

"I should've come here twenty years ago," said Al. He flipped the dice casually across the table and watched them rebound almost directly in front of him.

"Ten!" called the stickman. "Easy ten."

Joe smiled slowly. "Al, you're an artist." The dealer moved to give him his winnings, but Joe accepted only half the chips, saying, "Let the rest ride on the ten."

Again, Al threw the dice.

"Four!"

Attababy," said Joe. "Roll 'em again, champ." Once more, he turned to the Dealer and pushed forward a pile of chips. "Could you help out an old man and put these back on the four, please?"

"My pleasure," said the dealer. In craps, the dealers and stickmen always rooted for the customers, since the size of their tips depended on how much people won.

Al smoothed the hair at the back of his head. "I still don't understand how the hell this game works."

"It's better that way," said Joe. "Just keep rolling them numbers, and stay away from that seven!" He noticed that there was now a sizable crowd around the table.

Al tossed the dice.

"Nnn-nine!"

Again, the dealer pushed a pile of chips in Joe's direction. The woman across the table blew ecstatic kisses.

"Boy," said Al, shaking his head, "Willie would've loved this place, huh?"

"Yeah . . ." said Joe thoughtfully. He raised his eyes to the ceiling. "Hey, Willie! I hope you're watching all of this."

Al tapped him on the shoulder. "What are you talking about? He's the one who's probably setting it all up for us."

After an hour-and-a-half, they quit. Al's arm was so tired he had reverted to his initial form, when he tossed the dice now, they would barely reach the end of the table. *Enough is enough*, Joe thought. Abruptly, he scooped up his chips.

"Thank you, gents," he said, generously tipping the dealers and stickman. "Been a great pleasure."

"You sure you wanna leave?" said Al. "If I just massaged the arm a couple—"

"It's time," said Joe. "It's like they used to say about the stock market! Bulls make money. Bears make money. Pigs lose."

Al shrugged. "Except when they win. In which

case, no one calls them pigs. But . . . I ain't quarreling with the decision. Where to?"

"Cashier," said Joe.

As they started across the floor they were confronted by the enormous breasts of the woman who had stood opposite them at the table.

"Can I?" she said, looking down on them. Joe estimated her height, with heels, at six-foot-three.

"Can you what?" said Al.

"Give you a squeeze and a hug and a kiss for all you've done?"

"Can she?" said Al uncertainly.

"I believe it's within the law," said Joe.

The woman grabbed Al and cradled him in her arms. She kissed him forcefully on top of his head, leaving two perfect lipstick lips on his bald spot. Then it was Joe's turn. He found himself engulfed in overflowing flesh, his mouth and nose buried in the woman's fragrant cleavage. He felt her mouth press wetly on his forehead.

"Five years!" the woman squealed. "I've been betting these tables five years, and never have I had a night like tonight!"

"Me neither," said Joe.

"You're both dolls!" The woman blew them a kiss and pranced away.

"She reminded me of a gangster's girl friend," said Al. "I used to see a million of that type years ago."

"I bet she loses that money fast," speculated Joe.

Slowly, their eyes met. "Look at us," said Al. "Standin' here like we're judges, or somethin'. Us, who robbed a bank, and got a little lucky."

"What the hell," said Joe. "I ain't been kissed

like that in years. And if she wants to blow whatever she won, who's to say that ain't the best thing to do with it?"

Al nodded, and they headed again for the cashier's cage. The cashier, a woman, counted their chips at lightning speed, adding subtotals on a calculator. Her professionalism had a hypnotic, mind-lulling effect; Joe and Al did not even check the tally slip she pushed forward. "Twelve thousand, two hundred and seventy-five dollars," she said crisply.

"You hear that?" said Joe.

Al was watching two girls in tight pants who were bending over the roulette table. "Very nice," he said absentmindedly.

"Would you like cash, or would you prefer to leave it on deposit?" asked the cashier.

"That's an interesting question," said Joe. "I think maybe we'll leave it here with you for a while." He turned to Al. "That okay?"

"Sounds good to me," said Al.

# 14
# Like Thieves in the Night

The waitress, a leggy brunette in her late teens, stood awaiting their order. They were in the hotel coffee shop, and somehow the forty-minute wait for service had not disturbed them. Joe looked up from the menu. "Uh, listen, I don't see this here, but could I have a cream cheese and jelly sandwich, sweetheart?"

She smiled, almost.

"Cream cheese and jelly?"

"That's right."

"I'll ask them in back, sir. And do you want that on rye or white?"

"Rye'll be fine."

"Anything to drink?"

"Coffee is good," said Joe.

The waitress turned to Al. "And you, sir?"

Al folded the menu and handed it to her. "I'll have the same as him."

The waitress nodded, and left.

Joe watched her disappear into the kitchen. "Lotta good-looking women in this town."

"Yes, there are."

"After we eat, you wanna go to one of them naked girlie shows they got?"

Al yawned. "Ah, I dunno. I gotta think."

"What's to think?"

"I gotta decide whether I'm more interested in seeing naked women than in going to sleep."

"Yeah," agreed Joe reluctantly. "I guess I feel the same. Been a long day."

"Years ago," said Al, "I hardly needed any sleep at all. I could live for weeks on two, three hours a night."

"Maybe we're a little too old for this kind of nonsense," said Joe.

"Oh, let's not go *that* far," said Al.

The waitress brought their sandwiches and coffee. "I'll bet she's a student," said Joe, when she'd gone. "Works here in the summers to support herself at UCLA the rest of the year. Parents are probably dirt poor."

"You know somethin'?" said Al. "You're a worse romantic than I am."

They finished eating and stood up, brushing crumbs off their pants. The waitress had left their check on the table.

"You really think she's a student?" said Al.

"Yup. She got a certain sweetness you don't see in the real pro waitresses."

Al nodded. "Joe, is it all right with you if I leave a hundred dollar tip?"

196

"You're askin' the romantic for advice?"

"Just answer."

"Sure, it's all right," said Joe. "Why not? This is what money is for. Leave two hundred."

"Yeah?"

"Yeah."

"Two hundred dollars?"

"Ah, make it an even three hundred," said Joe. "You know what it costs to send a kid to college nowadays?"

Al counted out three hundred dollars and placed the bills under a glass on the table. "I always wanted to do that." As they headed for the cashier, he said, "I can't figure out what percent of the bill that is. I know it's more than the guide books usually recommend."

"Don't worry about it," said Joe. "She won't care if we've broken the guidelines."

While Joe was paying the check, Al started up with a very attractive woman in the lobby outside. She was wearing heavy, sequined eye makeup and her shorts were so cut off that the cheeks of her round behind peeked out. She smiled at Al, and he smiled back. Then she opened her mouth slightly and licked her lips. Al straightened his sport jacket. She turned sideways, thrust out her bosom and buttocks, and motioned with her head. Al walked over to her.

"Hi," he said pleasantly.

"Hi," said the woman. "How're you tonight, sweetie? Feelin' good?"

"Oh, I'm feeling fine," said Al. Since his back was to the coffee shop entrance, he did not see that Joe had come up behind him and was gesticulating wildly.

Joe, of course, had spotted the woman as a hooker, and he was trying to make her understand that his friend was not fair game.

"Wanna feel even better?" she said throatily to Al.

Al stood a little straighter, and raised his eyebrows. "What you got in mind?" he asked.

Her eyes skipped to Joe, who pointed at Al, then made little circles next to his own ear and shook his head in an emphatic "No." The hooker gave an almost imperceptible nod to show she understood.

"My suggestion is, find yourself a girl friend," she told Al. "A handsome man like you should have a woman alongside him to help live it up."

"How 'bout you?" said Al. "I mean, as long as you brought it up."

"I'd love to," she said, "but my husband would kill me." She blew him a kiss as she walked away. "Make some other chick happy, tiger, will you?"

Al watched her vanish around a corner, and Joe came up beside him. "What was that all about?"

"Beats me," said Al, "Some hooker, that's all. Tried to pick me up, then changed her mind for some reason."

"How'd you know she was a hooker?"

"Hey, come on, I was a bartender for years. If I say she was a hooker, you can put money on it." Al paused, his face wrinkling. "Which reminds me . . . You know, I never dreamed a place like this existed."

Joe looked at him, and slowly shook his head.

"What are you staring at?" demanded Al. "Never mind. Just get me to them tables! I'm feeling hot!"

In the casino, it was as it had been before. Same

198

craps table, same escalating winning streak, even many of the same spectators. Only the dealers and boxmen were new. After an hour, Joe and Al had a huge pile of chips in front of them, and huge piles riding on several numbers. As Al concentrated and shook the dice, the nearly twenty bettors and onlookers around the table were suddenly quiet. Al threw the dice firmly up against the far rail.

"Siiixxx!" chanted the stickman. "Easy six."

A loud cheer went up from the crowd. The dealer pushed an awesome pile of chips toward Joe and Al.

"I ain't never *ever* seen anything like this," said Joe.

"Even in France?" teased Al.

"Anywhere," said Joe. He turned to a large man next to him, a man wearing a Stetson hat and string tie. "Think we should quit, Tiny?"

Tiny had been one of their big boosters, laughing and matching them bet for bet. "Naw!" he said. "Soon you boys will be able to buy this joint. *That's* when you quit."

"Tiny says we shouldn't stop," Joe reported to Al.

"Gee, I dunno," said Al. "We're doin' pretty good here now." He ran his fingers down a stack of chips. "How much you figure we got?"

Joe shook his head. "I stopped counting around twenty minutes ago, and back then it was a little over thirty grand."

"Thir*ty?* Or thir*teen?*"

"Thirty, Al, and that don't include the twelve grand from before."

Al exhaled through puckered lips. "Holy Moses!" he muttered.

"I know," said Joe. He saw that all the people

around the table, including the casino employees, were staring at him unashamedly. He could only nod politely and smile. Finally the stickman said, "Will you be rolling again, sir?"

Joe slowly shook his head, Yes. He turned to Al. "Let's go for one more throw, then cash in our chips and see what's going on."

"I don't know I—"

"Stay with me on this, all right?" said Joe. "I got a feeling."

"All right," Al agreed reluctantly. "Whatever you say."

Joe turned to the dealer. "Let's take all those bets off the numbers . . . ah . . . except, let's see . . . leave five hundred on the eight and . . . uh . . . five hundred on the six."

The dealer obeyed. Joe recalled with amusement how tentative he and Al had been with their first bets. And now here they were commanding the hushed attention of employees and spectators alike. The stickman shoved the dice toward Al, who, with a swift, practiced movement, banked them easily off the opposite rail.

"Sssevvv-en!" called the stickman.

As the losing bets were cleared off the felt, Joe offered Tiny his hand. "That's it," he said, smiling.

"You boys are okay," said Tiny. "You ever down around Austin, you look me up."

Joe and Al passed out small piles of chips to each of the dealers, the stickman, and the boxman. "Here you go, gentlemen," said Joe.

"Thank you, sir," came the replies.

"Buy yourselves some hats," Al called back, as he and Joe carried their chips toward the cashier's window.

"Get ready to be rich," said Joe out of the side of his mouth.

For the second time that night, they waited anxiously while the woman in the office ran up numbers on the calculator. When she looked up, her face betrayed no emotion at all. "These total sixty thousand and nine hundred dollars," she said. "Would you like to have a check now, or shall I simply credit your account."

Joe said shakily, "Just, uh, credit our account. For now." He took the receipt she was holding out to him, started away, then stopped suddenly and whirled. "How late are you open tonight?"

The cashier smiled. "We never close, sir."

"Never close . . ."

"No, sir."

Joe nodded. "That's good," he said. "Good policy."

● ● ● ●

Back in their room, Al flopped down on the bed. "Oh, that feels good. I could sleep for twelve hours. I figure we'll wake up late, have us a nice big breakfast. Then, maybe about twelve, one, in the afternoon we can go back in the casino."

Joe paced. "We gotta get outta here right away."

"What? Why?"

"Why? You heard the number that cashier gave us?"

"Yeah, I heard." Al sat up. "What's that come to, countin' the money we won before?"

"A little over seventy-three grand," said Joe, emphasizing each syllable.

"So why's that mean we gotta leave?"

201

"Because that much money is serious stuff," said Joe. "Some of them bums downstairs are gonna try and rob us, or the FBI'll wanna know who the old guys are."

"Bums? What bums?"

"Al," said Joe patiently. "This town has two classes of people. The suckers and the suckees. Half the audience at our table were Mafia men, hustlers, confidence boys, call girls, and other assorted low-lifes—and the other half was there to keep an eye on them."

"I think you're bein' dramatic," said Al. "Goin' off the deep end."

"Al, believe me, there are guys around who weigh three hundred pounds and have little button pig eyes that don't even blink when they grind their heels into people like you and me. I'm telling you, they're around. You worked in bars all those years? Explain to me the line between bouncers and muggers."

"A bouncer is an employed mugger," said Al. "but I still don't see what the FBI has to do with it."

"I read in the paper once where they hang out in joints like this, looking for crooks. A lot of people don't declare gambling winnings on their income tax."

"So, we'll declare them." said Al. "What are we, criminals?"

"Bank robbery is a federal crime. Any bank has federal funds. I assure you, they're looking for us."

Al stood up. Tired as he was, he had nevertheless been convinced. "So what do we do?"

"We gotta get our money and get the hell out of here."

At the gift shop in the lobby, they bought a

brown leather satchel. Then they went back to the casino cashier's window. Joe plopped the satchel down on the tiny counter. "Hi," he said. "Remember us?"

"Yes, sir," said the cashier, her voice showing no trace of either pleasure or displeasure.

Joe pulled the receipt from his pocket and passed it to her. "We'd like to pick up our money."

"Okay." The cashier motioned toward a couch against the wall. "Why don't you both have a seat over there while I have a check drawn up."

Joe cleared his throat loudly. "Uh, we'd prefer it in cash . . . if you can."

"For these amounts, sir, we usually draw out a corporate check. It's quite safe."

"I'm sure," said Joe. "Nevertheless—"

"It's practically the same as a teller's check. If there's a problem, your bank can even phone us and verify directly that—"

"We'd really kinda like the cash," persisted Joe.

The cashier pursed her lips. She was a fiftyish, platinum blonde with a hardened, plaster-of-paris face. She wore a black uniform on which a flap above a blouse pocket advised, *Live It Up.* "Uh . . . okay. Could both of you wait just a minute?"

"Sure," said Joe.

The cashier disappeared through a door at the back of the office. A few minutes later, she returned with a tall man with steel-gray hair, wearing a tuxedo. The man stooped slightly in order to peer out the cage at Joe and Al. "Good evening, gentlemen. I'm Jim Chambers, the casino manager."

"How do you do," said Joe.

"I'd like to congratulate you on your luck."

"Well, that's very nice of you. Thank you."

"It's a beautiful place you got here," added Al.

The manager smiled. "Now, what seems to be the problem?"

Joe shrugged. "No problem here."

"These gentlemen have a little over seventy-three thousand on deposit," explained the cashier. "They'd like to take it with them in cash."

Chambers nodded. "Ah, I see. Well, of course, if you want it, we certainly will oblige."

"Good," said Joe. "Then we're all set."

"However," added Chambers, "I really don't think it's the wisest way to go about it."

"Don't worry," said Joe. "It's okay." He patted the leather satchel. "We just bought this, and it's got a lock on it, see?"

"Is it the corporate check that's worrying you?" said Chambers. "Because, if that's the problem, we can arrange for a bank check tomorrow morning. It's really—"

"The thought hadn't crossed my mind," said Joe. He turned to Al. "Did that bother you?"

"Not me," said Al.

"What about wire?" said Chambers.

"Wire is strong," said Joe, "but I think the lock holds the bag shut even better."

"No, I mean we could wire the money direct to your bank."

"I don't think ours has a wire service," said Joe.

Chambers lowered his voice. "There is a service the casino provides. . . . Usually, it's limited to people who've won more than a hundred thousand, but, perhaps we could make an arrangement. It works like this. You go home with your receipt. You live in a large city?"

"New York."

"Fine. At a mutually convenient time, our courier meets you in the lobby of your bank. He hands you a briefcase with the cash, you give him the receipt. You can then stash the money in your safe deposit box, or do whatever else you like with it." Chambers grinned. "Naturally, the casino hopes you'll return here and lose it back to us. We just want to make it as easy as possible for you to do so." He waited, eyes listening.

"Mr. Chambers," said Joe slowly, "that is a very lovely offer. You're really fine people here, absolutely terrific. But if it's all the same to you, my friend and I would still like the cash."

Chambers raised his eyebrows. "Up to you."

"See, the main problem," volunteered Al, "is that we don't trust banks."

● ● ● ●

Back in their room, a sense of urgency drove them.

"I don't know why the hell we're killin' ourselves," said Al, as they emptied the dresser drawers. "I mean, even the muggers would need some time to plan how to get us."

"It's just instinct," said Joe. "Same as when we were shootin' craps. I have this intuition that if we ain't outta here by tonight, we'll never make it. I feel the hairs on my neck standin' up."

"Mine are too thin to stand up," said Al. "And too tired. I'm too exhausted to even collapse."

"Just hold on," said Joe. "Another couple hours, we're home free." He unlocked the leather bag and

205

dumped packages of hundred-dollar bills all over the bed, then stuffed a rolled-up shirt and several pairs of socks into the satchel. "This look okay?"

"Unless they got X-ray vision, yeah," said Al.

Joe locked the bag and watched Al finish cramming clothing and toiletries into their old suitcase. Then both men began stuffing their underwear and pockets with the stacks of hundreds.

"My shorts alone are worth a Cadillac," said Al. "My undershirt could get you a mortgage on a small house."

"Just try to look natural," said Joe.

"How can I look natural when I got all this money interferin' with my privates?" said Al.

In the lobby, Joe carried the leather bag, his knuckles white with tension, while a bellhop walked ahead with their light suitcase. The bellhop waited while Al paid the bill at the desk, and then they all started out. They had almost reached the front door when a voice rang out behind them. "Hey, y'all, how're ya doin'?"

Joe looked back and saw Tiny, the Texan who'd been in the casino. He waved, but kept walking. "Get us a cab, quick," he told the bellhop through clenched teeth. A moment later they were outside, but Tiny and an equally large friend had followed them out.

The bellhop put their suitcase into the trunk of a waiting taxi. "Can I take this, sir?" he asked, indicating the leather satchel.

"No," said Joe. "No." He jerked open the cab's door, and waited while Al climbed inside. He felt a meaty hand on his shoulder.

"Hey, cuz, where you runnin'?" said Tiny. "Me

and Lucas here, we're throwin' us a little party. Thought maybe you'd like to come."

"Uh, no, thanks," said Joe. "We have a plane to catch."

Tiny guffawed. "Aw, you don't gotta worry 'bout no plane. Not with what you won today. Besides, them things run all night. Whyn't you come back with us, an' have yourself some fun? We're havin' booze, girls, the works. Whaddaya say?"

"Sorry," said Joe. He tried to step into the cab, but the hand on his shoulder was gripping tighter now. Also, he felt a strong tug on the satchel.

"Hey, what's this, yore winnin's? You ain't takin' home all that money in this l'il ol' bag now, is you?"

Joe jerked himself free and scrambled into the cab. He saw Al lean out the window on the opposite side and say something to the bellhop, who then signaled the doorman. The doorman came forward, interposed himself between Tiny and the taxi, and firmly closed the door. "Have a pleasant trip," he said, and the cab began to move.

Joe closed his eyes and slumped against the back of the seat. He shuddered.

"Airport, please," Al told the driver, and the cab picked up speed.

Joe shook his head. "Just tell me what you said to that bellhop," he mumbled.

"Just asked him if he'd get someone to shut the door for a tired old man," Al said with theatrical innocence. "Anyone would've done the same as he did—especially for the hundred-dollar bill I handed him."

Joe glanced out the rear window. "Well, at least

207

we ain't being followed. So far, anyway. That's a good sign."

Al yawned broadly. "I still think you're exaggeratin' everything. Personally, I think maybe we should've spent the night. I am absolutely bushed."

"Believe me," said Joe, "this is the best way."

"It's the best way only if I live through it."

"You'll live," said Joe. "You can get some sleep on the plane."

"Are you kidding? I can sooner fall asleep on a roller coaster. I don't like them jets."

"You wanna go anywhere today," Joe told him, "you gotta adjust to modern inventions. Any country that can put a man on the moon can fly two old geezers back from Las Vegas."

Al looked out the window. "I don't care. I don't trust no plane that ain't got propellers."

● ● ● ●

Forty minutes later they were airborne. Al looked down at the glowing, coruscating jewel beneath them that was nighttime Las Vegas. He sighed. "Boy, I'd like to come back here sometime. I really would."

"We will," said Joe. "We can do whatever we want now. We're free as birds." He leaned back. He heard the steady drone of the engines, felt their slight, but steady vibration. It was actually quite relaxing if you could put aside the newness of it all, forget the fact that you were in a thin-walled metal container, thirty-five thousand feet up, hurtling at six hundred miles per hour through the rarefied, freezing night air. Eliminate those considerations and a man could nod right off, he thought. Miss the meal, the movie, and everything else. . . .

Joe awoke just as they touched down, the wheels bumping and screeching on the runway, bright sunlight streaming in the windows. He turned sleepily toward Al, who was sitting bolt upright. "What time is it?"

Al looked at him. "So . . . sleeping beauty awakes, huh? You missed the whole thing."

"What? Where are we?"

The plane slowed and made a wide turn. "Where do you think?"

"Kennedy?"

"That's right. Kennedy."

"I can't believe it."

Al shook his head. "I can't understand how a human bein' can just conk out the way you done. Either you got nerves of steel, or half a brain, and I'll be damned if I can tell which."

In the taxi, on their way into New York City from JFK, Joe kept glancing out the rear window. "We're still okay," he said happily. "There ain't no one behind us."

"Jesus," said Al, "I can hardly keep my eyes open."

"Why don't you take some more of them vitamins?"

Al managed a weak smile. "Yeah. 'I'm sure they'd fix me right up."

Joe noticed that Al's mouth seemed to be sort of hanging open, and that his eyelids were fluttering uncontrollably. "Just hold on a little while longer," he pleaded.

"I'm holdin'," said Al. "I'm holdin'."

"We're almost there."

Joe tipped the cabbie two dollars when they came to a stop in front of their apartment building. "Funny," he said as the taxi pulled away, "it was all I could do to stop myself from givin' him a hundred. Amazin' how your values change."

"Mmm." Al was practically semiconscious.

"Come on," said Joe, picking up both the leather satchel and the suitcase. "We'll go upstairs."

In the hall outside their apartment. Al leaned against a wall while Joe fumbled with his keys. At last the lock tumblers clicked, the knob was turned, and the door swung slowly open.

"That's it, Al," said Joe. "We made it."

# 15
## The Sky's the Limit

Al lay on the bed. Next to him was a large pile of hundred-dollar bills. In a nearby chair, Joe too relaxed. They were both in their underwear.

"You look like one of them Arab sheiks," said Joe. "A chintzy one, of course. The real biggies would be lyin' next to a pile of gold."

Al winced as he shifted position. One side of his face seemed strangely slack. "The real biggies have girls in veils massaging their tootsies. And they lay in pools of oil."

"Well, maybe that's next," said Joe. "There's no stoppin' us now, you know. It's like they say: Money comes to money. The sky's the limit."

Al grunted. "Jesus, I feel like I've been beat up."

Joe's voice was dreamy. "You were great back there, Al. The best."

"I had a good time. I was lucky, and I took advantage of it."

"I betcha them guys never saw nobody roll like that before."

Al forced a smile. "You weren't doin' too bad yourself, kid."

"Ah, I did nothin'. The whole thing is how you throw the dice. That takes the talent, the rest is mechanical."

"Never mind," said Al. "Movin' those chips around is what got us all that money. Mechanical, my ass. That takes smarts. I could study that game for a million years and still not know the right way to play."

"Don't worry about it," said Joe. "On our next gamblin' outing, you'll do the betting and I'll roll. Maybe we'll try Monte Carlo, or the French Riviera. Or—hey!—how do the Bahamas strike you?"

"I need sleep," said Al.

Joe nodded. "Funny, it's like we've lived two lives. One before the robbery and one after."

Al's eyes were closing. "I think I like the one after better."

"Me, too." Joe's own lids were drooping. "Me, too."

When Joe shook himself awake, it was dark outside. A blue light shone eerily into the bedroom. Al was still asleep next to the pile of money. Joe padded slowly into the kitchen. Damn, he thought. I'm missing entire days and nights out of my life, and not keeping track of where they're going. He turned on the radio, put a teapot full of water on the stove, then went into the bathroom to rinse his face. The splash of coldness refreshed him. He toweled himself off, then returned to the kitchen, where the teapot was already whistling. He poured hot water into two cups and dunked a teabag in one until the liquid was a deep yellow-brown. He was about to transfer the bag when he stopped. Nuts to that, he thought. That was what poor people did. He removed a fresh teabag from the box and put it into the second cup. *That's* how we live from now on, he thought.

A voice on the radio caught his attention. "Last Thursday's senior citizen robbery of the Union Marine Bank still seems to be capturing everyone's interest," said the announcer. "Although the FBI is maintaining its traditional silence, a spokesman for the Police Department said today that new developments in the case would be breaking shortly, due to the abundance of traceable clues left behind."

"What?" Joe positioned himself directly opposite the radio. "What clues? You ain't got no clues."

"Inspector Edward McClusky," the announcer went on, "has characterized the robbers as, quote, a careless group of amateurs, unquote, and promised the investigation would quickly lead to indictments."

"Indictments!" Joe shouted. "You don't even know who the hell we are or where we went." He turned the dial abruptly to a different station. "Stupid asses," he muttered.

He took the two cups of tea and carried them into Al's bedroom. "Al," he said firmly. "Wake up. Come on, kid, you been alseep for ten hours now, that should be plenty." He set one of the cups down on the night table and switched on the light. "Damn FBI," he continued. "I can't believe it. After all we done, they still call us a bunch of amateurs."

He sat down and sipped his tea, waiting for Al

to awaken. "I suppose you gotta knock off a bank every other week in order to get some respect from those jerks." He shook his head. "Hey, Al, come on."

Al remained motionless. His mouth was agape, his body rigid.

"Al, your tea's gonna get cold."

A heaviness began to spread through Joe's chest. "If you keep sleeping," he said hesitantly, "your whole schedule will get all turned around." He forced himself to take another sip of tea. "Believe me, I know what I'm talking about."

Joe rose, his jaws tightening until he thought the muscles would burst. "Al?" He approached the bed and reached out to touch his friend's shoulder. "Al, come on now."

Still no movement.

"Come on now, wake up! *Wake up!* WAKE UP! YOU HEAR ME? WAKE UP!" Joe felt his throat constrict from the effort of his shouting. He bent and placed his ear to Al's chest. He could hear nothing. He probed without success for a pulse in Al's wrist, then his temple. There was no sign of respiration, no rise and fall of the rib cage.

Joe felt his own head become light; it seemed to detach itself and float away. He stumbled back to the chair and cradled his forehead in one gnarled hand.

"It's just not fair," he said aloud. "I mean, what's going on here? Everytime I turn my back, one of you guys is dropping dead on me."

He watched Al for a long time, perhaps as much as a half hour. Then he leaned forward and pulled the cover over his friend's head.

●　●　●　●

After two more cups of tea, Joe felt he'd re-gained sufficient composure. Life had to go on. No sense losing everything they'd worked for. Besides, he had both Willie *and* Al looking down and watch-ing him now. If he screwed up, there'd be hell to pay when it came time to join them.

Joe collected all the money from Al's bed and put it in a paper shopping bag. Then he called Ryan's Funeral Home and told them about Al. Ryan was more expensive than Bender, but at least he'd spare you the crap about his father being buried in cherrywood. A Mr. Longwood answered the phone, and explained that Ryan had gone home for the night.

"My friend is dead," said Joe. "Does that mean I gotta wait for tomorrow before someone picks up the body?"

"No, no, not at all," said Longwood. "Just give me the address, we'll send a man over."

Joe gave him the address.

"You'll have the doctor there with the death cer-tificate?" Longwood asked.

Joe was taken aback. "Uh, no, there is no . . . Well, I mean, a doctor hasn't seen him."

"You gotta have a doctor," said Longwood.

"Well, we don't use anyone steady," said Joe. "And besides, who's gonna come to the house?"

"I'll arrange something," said Longwood. "We have some medical people who work with us."

An hour later, three men knocked on Joe's door. Two of them were curly-haired and Italian-looking; the third was tiny, bald, and abrupt. "Dr. Feigen-baum," he said briskly, offering Joe a limp hand. "Where's the deceased?"

215

"Inside," said Joe.

They all walked into Al's bedroom. Feigenbaum pulled a stethoscope from his black bag and checked various points on Al's body. After two minutes, he looked up. "This man is dead," he declared crisply.

"I know that," said Joe.

Feigenbaum withdrew a sheet of paper from his bag. "Happened about an hour ago, you say?"

"Yes."

"We'll put time of death at, mmm, nine-twenty-three," said the doctor, peering at his watch before he wrote. "Cause could be anything. Hard to tell. He have any immediate family?"

"Immediate? No," said Joe.

Feigenbaum shrugged. "Then it doesn't matter. We'll put down heart failure."

"His face was sort of saggin' on one side before he fell asleep," said Joe. "That mean somethin'?"

Feigenbaum shrugged. "Could be. Could be a stroke. Who knows? We'll leave the heart failure, though. I don't like to erase or cross out."

They returned to the kitchen, where Joe had to sign some papers authorizing the funeral home to remove the body. Then the two curly-haired men brought in a stretcher and carried out Al's remains.

"My condolences," said Feigenbaum without feeling, at the door.

"Thanks," said Joe. He waited five minutes after the men had left, then grabbed the shopping bag with the money and started out.

Mrs. Flaum poked her head out the door of her apartment. "Something wrong?"

"Nope," said Joe.

"I heard voices."

"TV, maybe," said Joe.

"Also footsteps."

"Maybe someone's following you," said Joe.

"It wasn't by me, the footsteps, it was by you." She was in the hall now, an apparition in pink curlers and a shapeless housedress. "Listen, late night visitors and wild parties are not the sort of thing we encourage here." Her hands were on her hips.

Joe smiled sweetly. "Mrs. Flaum, go to hell!" He walked past her, ignoring her rantings and threats.

Outside, the night air was humid and absolutely still. Joe felt himself being bitten by innumerable mosquitoes as he plodded along the darkened streets. Crazy, he thought. Absolutely crazy. Of the three, he was the oldest and the weakest, and here they were dead, while he still kept going. God had played an elaborate joke, worked a fine irony at his expense. At age seventy-eight he was finally rich, independent, able to grant himself any indulgence. Only what could he do? Youth was wasted on the young, and money on the old.

When he came to the house, he hesitated a moment before the tiny, almost bare lawn, then walked down the patched concrete path to the door. He knocked softly, and was surprised at how promptly the door was opened.

"Joe!" said Pete. "How you doin'? C'mon in."

"Thanks." Joe stepped inside, carrying the paper bag under one arm.

Colleen waved to him from the living room where she and Kevin were watching TV. "Hello, Joe!"

"Hiya, beautiful." Joe turned to Pete. "Kinda late for the kids to be up, no?"

"Yeah, I suppose. But you know, it's Kevin's last free week before school starts, so we figured we'd give him a break. And Colleen won't go to sleep unless he does, so that's that."

"I guess kids deserve their fling like anyone else," said Joe. "You can't be a tyrant."

"Well, we try to strike a balance," said Pete. "I'm the easy one, Kath is the tough one." He looked over Joe's shoulder. "Al didn't come along?"

"No, he's at home," said Joe. "I just came over to talk to you about some stuff."

"Sure, always glad to have you." For a moment, Pete's face tensed. "There's nothing wrong, is there?"

"No."

Kathy looked in from the kitchen. "Joe . . . how are you?"

"Hi, Kathy. I'm fine, thanks. Yourself?"

"Oh, not bad. I've been trying to sew something on this old machine I have, and one of the wheels keeps falling off. My husband, the mechanic, offered to fix it, but so far . . . nothing." She grinned.

"I'll get to it, I'll get to it," said Pete. "My one night off, I've gotta relax a little first."

"Up to you," said Kathy breezily. "It's your pants I'm sewing, so if you don't mind everyone admiring your undershorts, it's fine with me."

"I don't mind," said Pete.

"Joe," said Kathy, "you look kinda tired. Would you like a cup of coffee or something?"

"No, thanks." Joe changed his mind. "Yeah . . . on second thought, if you already got some made."

"Kathy, is there any coffee made?" asked Pete.

"No, but it'll just take a second."

Joe nodded. "He'll have," said Pete.

218

"Fine." Kathy returned to the kitchen.

"Is there somewhere we can go to talk alone?" Joe asked Pete.

"Sure. Come on."

They walked down the steps to the basement, Joe holding the banister with one hand, the bag with the other.

"Years ago," said Pete, "I was gonna put a bar down here, planned to build it myself." He shrugged. "One of those things you have in the back of your head, until you finally realize you're never gonna do it."

They sat down at a small bridge table. "Pete," said Joe, "I want you to promise me that you'll never say a word to anybody about what I'm going to tell you."

Pete grinned. "So serious, my God. What'd you do, murder somebody? Rob a bank?"

"I mean it, Pete. Nothing to nobody unless you check with me first. Unless you agree, we may as well go back upstairs."

The grin vanished. "Yeah, okay. You have my word of honor, Joe."

Joe leaned forward. "Just before, when you thought maybe I was kiddin', you asked me two questions. The answer to the first—did I murder somebody—is no." He paused. "But the answer to the second—is yes."

Pete's face was uncomprehending. "You mean—"

"We robbed a bank. Me, Willie, and your uncle Al."

Pete shook his head. "No. Hey, Joe, come on. What are you telling me here? This is crazy."

219

"You heard in the news about the Union Marine Bank? How it was held up by three senior citizens?"

"Yeah, but—"

"We hired a gypsy cab in Corona. We bought disguises. We went back by subway. It couldn't've gone more perfect if we'd spent twenty years planning it instead of twenty minutes."

Pete's face was twisted in incredulity. "You mean—wait a minute. That was you three guys? Are you bullshitting me?"

"This is no bullshit," said Joe.

Pete's expression changed gradually to one of stunned acceptance. "I can't believe it. I hear what you're saying but—it's fantastic! Unreal!"

"That's only the half of it," said Joe.

"You mean, there's more? I don't know if I can stand the shock."

"There's a lot more, and you'll have to stand it." Joe forced himself to continue. "Right after we buried Willie, me and your uncle took off to Las Vegas for a couple of hours and cleaned those bums out for over seventy thousand."

Pete's eyes seemed about to fly from his skull. "Did you say seventy or seven*teen*?"

"Seventy. Seven zero."

"My God. . . ."

Joe turned over the paper bag and dumped a mound of hundred-dollar bills on the table. "Between the bank job and Vegas, the total comes to a little over a hundred six thousand dollars."

Pete stared at the pile of money, mesmerized as much by its physical presence as by the manner in which it had been acquired.

"It was actually a couple of thousand more, but

220

we spent some of it in the hotel and for plane fares . . . and, of course, there was Willie's funeral." Joe paused. "Which brings me to the next subject. Pete—"

"Jesus," whispered Pete, "Jesus. Holy . . . Jesus."

"Pete—"

"Who would believe this?"

"Pete!"

Pete looked up.

"Al's dead," said Joe.

"What?"

"Al died a couple of hours ago."

"What? What're you saying?"

"Pete, believe me, I am so sorry to break all of this to you this way, but things are coming to a head, and it has to be done."

"Al's dead?" said Pete dazedly. The meaning of the words, the depth and utter finality, had not yet sunk in.

"We came back from Las Vegas this afternoon," said Joe, "and we were real tired. Al especially. We hardly got any sleep since before the funeral, and what with all the excitement and everything, it must've been too much for him. As soon as we got home, we both nodded off right away. Later, I woke up, but he . . . must've died in his sleep."

"Oh, God . . ."

"The doctor said most likely his heart just stopped." Joe sighed. "There was no pain or nothin'. He just . . . didn't wake up."

Kathy's voice came from upstairs. "Pete and Joe—coffee's ready."

Pete inhaled and sat up. "We'll be there in a minute, honey," he called.

"You want me to bring it down?"

"No, that's okay. We'll be up soon." A single tear trickled out of one of Pete's eyes and down his cheek. "Where is he?" he whispered to Joe.

"I called Ryan's Funeral Home before I came over. Everything's taken care of."

Pete covered his face with his hands. "Jesus, how am I gonna tell the kids? Both my father and Kathy's died before they were born—he was like a Grandpa to them."

"Look," said Joe, "I know this whole thing is rough on you, but you gotta pull yourself together and listen to me for a minute."

Pete nodded shakily, then took several deep breaths. "All right, go ahead."

"When me, Al, and Willie pulled the bank job, we didn't know what the hell we were doing."

"But you said you planned it. It sounded like—"

"I know what it sounded like, and at the time we thought we were pretty smart . . . but we were wrong. We were stupid. We just ran in and did it. Now I've been hearing stuff on the radio and thinking about how we approached this thing, and I got the feeling we loused up somehow."

"You think they're closing in?" said Pete.

"I dunno. Maybe."

"But what tipped them off? How could they possibly trace you?"

Joe shook his head. "Can't tell. I just got this feeling. . . ."

"What are you gonna do?"

"I don't know. What I need from you, Pete, is somewhere to stash all of this money. If there's trouble, at least I know one thing is taken care of."

"I'm with you, Joe. Whatever I can do."

"Good. You got one of them safe deposit boxes?"

Pete squinted at the mass of bills on the table. Yeah, I do, but it's not gigantic. I just use it to keep some papers in—the mortgage, insurance, that kind of thing."

"You think it'll hold all this?"

Pete managed a faint smile. "I think I can squeeze it in."

"You're a good kid," said Joe appreciatively. "I want you to take care of this right away, first thing in the morning."

"Nine a.m.," said Pete. "Soon as the bank opens."

"And something else," said Joe. "You gotta promise me that if anything should happen, you won't turn any of this dough over to the cops."

"You have my word, Joe."

"It would just bring you trouble, and them bastards would probably wind up taking all of it. They'd assume it was all stolen."

"They'll never see any of it, Joe."

Joe looked at him. "You understand, don't you, that this makes you an accessorary to the crime?"

"Accessory," corrected Pete. "Yeah, I understand that. Don't worry."

They stood up. "All right then," Joe said. "I'm gonna get going." He extended his hand, and Pete cupped it in both his own. "You won't stay for coffee?"

Joe shook his head. "You drink it with Kathy, and you tell her what's what. A man shouldn't keep secrets from his wife. I remember—1933, I think it was—I put my entire savings in the stock market, figured it'd bottom out. When I lost it, I didn't tell

Myrna. I was too ashamed. The thing was, I forgot about the money in a couple of weeks—I mean, it's just paper—but my not tellin' Myrna, the guilt stayed with me for years. Years." He tapped Pete on the shoulder. "So you tell Kathy everything, hear? It's her risk too."

"I'll tell her," said Pete. "I would've anyway, whether you asked me to or not."

"Good. Now . . . Al stashed the dough from the robbery in some suitcase he keeps here. You know where that is?"

Pete shrugged. "It's not hard to figure out. He only *had* one piece of luggage, and he kept that in the closet down here."

"All right," said Joe. "You take care of that after I leave."

They walked toward the foot of the staircase. "You're a hell of a guy, Joe."

"Never mind that. I just wish my friends had lived to share a little while longer in the good fortune." Joe closed his eyes. "I guess it just wasn't meant to be."

"You take care of *your*self now, Joe. Take it real easy, rest up."

"I will. Just remember, no matter what happens, do exactly like I told you, Pete. I got your word."

"You do, Joe, and it's good. Don't worry about me. I'll do just like you say."

Joe nodded. "Okay. I'll see you at Ryan's in the morning."

Kathy met them at the top of the steps. "Well, you two, about time. I was just coming down. I think you have iced coffee by now, instead of regular."

"Kath," said Joe. "I'm afraid I'm gonna have to disappoint you. I have to be leavin'."

"Oh, Joe—"

"No, really. I'm sorry, but tomorrow's gonna be a very heavy day for me."

"But surely one cup—" Pete's hand on her arm made her fall silent.

"Pete'll explain everything," said Joe. "And really, thanks for the hospitality. I'll come see you again when I got more time. I know I'm a terrible guest."

At the front door, Kathy said, "Joe, you sure Pete can't give you a ride home? It's no trouble."

"She's right," said Pete.

"No, no, I'll walk." Joe stepped outside. "Just forgive me my awful manners, will you?"

"You're always welcome here, you know that," Kathy called through the screen. Then, as he trudged down the concrete path: "Give our regards to Al, will you?"

"Sure," said Joe, in a voice so low she couldn't possibly have heard. "Sure."

When he got back to the apartment, he put on some hot water for tea, then changed his mind and shut off the burner. He went into Al's room, opened the closet door and took out a few pairs of trousers and some shirts. The place would have to be cleaned, the old clothes donated to the Salvation Army. May as well start now, get a jump. . . .

Joe closed the door and returned to the kitchen. Impulsively, he pounded on the table. Noise! Noise meant life. Any noise—breathing, nose-blowing, farting, skin-scratching—meant there was another presence, another being close by to relieve the loneliness.

But now there was only silence—and there would be only silence.

"What the hell should I do?" said Joe aloud. "Get a dog?"

Al's not dead four hours and already I'm talking to myself, he thought. He sat down on a chair and stared at the light. He knew it was futile to go to bed; sleep would come hard this evening. After a while, he folded his hands in front of him and sat that way for the better part of the night.

# 16
## Game Over

*Scraping*. Razor blade on parched, papier-mâ-ché, seventy-eight-year-old skin.

Joe stood in front of the bathroom mirror in black pants and sleeveless undershirt. Years ago, his son had given him an electric razor, touting it highly. Why go through the whole business with the shaving cream? he'd asked. And the skill pulling, and buying new blades all the time, and disposing of the old ones, and having to wash the razor, and dry it, and using the styptic pencil, or bits of toilet paper. . . ? Joe had agreed to try the electric razor, but had discarded it after two days. His son had missed the point. It was no good simply because it failed to use up enough time.

After coffee, Joe put on a white shirt and then a

black tie. It was still only 8 a.m., way too early for Al's funeral, and yet . . . Joe couldn't stay indoors. The apartment was oppressive, crowded with silence and packed-in memories. He grabbed his suit jacket from a hall closet, took one last look around to see that everything was in order, and stepped out the door. Once again he had that peculiar tingling in his spine, the tingling he'd felt in Las Vegas when he'd removed most of his bets from the table, and then they'd lost. . . .

Outside, the bright sun made him squint. The day was perfect—clear, low humidity, the air fresh. Across the street, he saw three small children dressed in light jackets, carrying little briefcases. One of them had a name tag pinned to her, unreadable, of course, from this distance. Joe could not help smiling, and then a surprisingly intense feeling swept over him: *I want to go with you. I want to be back in school and have it all happen again.* And then, suddenly, a man stood before him, a serious, sober-faced man who flashed something from his wallet that said, FBI. The man gripped Joe tightly on the arm. Two more men appeared behind him; they stepped forward and roughly pinned Joe's hands at the small of his back, then snapped cold metal cuffs around his wrists. They pushed him over to the side of a building, leaned him against the brick, and began to run their hands over his body.

"He's clean," said the tallest of the agents, a blond.

From the corner of his eye, Joe saw the three children climb aboard a school bus. Strangely, what was happening to him seemed of little interest or

228

importance. It was the children who occupied his thoughts. He was with them on their way to school; he would tell them not to be afraid, that kindergarten or first grade or second really wasn't all that bad, that you made things and learned things, and came home to Mommy in the afternoon. It was a good time in one's life, a very good time.

Four husky agents, guns drawn, emerged from a car and ran toward Joe's apartment building. Onlookers began to gather, as Joe was allowed to straighten up and turn around. A police car drew up to the curb, and then another, this one squealing to a melodramatic stop. A half-dozen uniformed policemen took up positions near the house.

"Your friends still inside?" the blond agent asked Joe.

"You're too late," said Joe. "They've left for a better climate."

The blond motioned to a hawk-faced agent, who led Joe to a blue Plymouth and accompanied him into the back seat. Wide-eyed children and mothers wearing curlers drew closer, staring. The agent began to read from a small card: "Joseph Harris, we arrest you for the crime of robbery committed against the Union Marine Bank on September 5, 1979. You have the right to remain silent, the right to consult a . . ."

Joe's mind began to wander. He winked and made faces at several of the children. Mrs. Flaum appeared at the door of the building and called out to him. "Mr. Harris! Hey! Mr. Harris! What's going on here?"

FBI agents streamed out of the building behind her, their guns holstered now.

"Mistaken identity," called Joe, smiling. "They got the wrong man."

An agent got into the front of the Plymouth and started the motor.

"Anything?" asked the hawk-faced man next to Joe.

The driver shook his head, and they pulled away from the curb.

Joe said, "Al, Willie—that's it. They nabbed us."

"What?" said the hawk-faced man.

"Who's talking to you?" said Joe.

They rode rapidly through the city streets. Joe felt sorry for Mrs. Flaum, but at the same time he couldn't help being amused—the FBI agents would tear their apartment to shreds in search of the money; the landlady would give them a lifetime supply of verbal abuse. He was still imagining the details of the confrontation when the car pulled up before a three-story, white stone building on Queens Boulevard.

The agents ushered Joe through a crowd of reporters and photographers, several of whom shouted questions, but Joe was inside before he could think of answers. He was led rapidly through marble-tiled corridors, then up a flight of stairs, through a big room where perhaps a dozen people sat at dilapidated wooden desks, and finally into a smaller room that held only a table, two chairs, and a row of file cabinets. Searching through one of the open drawers was a neatly dressed young man with hard, brown eyes. He looked up as Joe entered. "Any problems?" he asked the blond and hawk-face, both of whom still accompanied Joe.

The blond motioned him into a corner, and there was a tense, whispered interchange. Then the

230

blond unlocked Joe's handcuffs, and left with the hawk-face agent, closing the door behind them.

"I'm Richard Tuffo," said the hard-eyed man. "I've been heading the investigation of your case."

"Very nice," said Joe.

"Joe, I'd like to spend a moment explaining what will happen to you in the next few hours and days. After we're through here, you'll be formally booked downstairs for the crime with which you're charged. It's a very serious crime, Joe, I hope you understand that."

Joe shrugged.

"You'll be asked for information on your background and occupation; you'll be fingerprinted and photographed. Then you'll be brought back for formal questioning, during which you are entitled to have a lawyer present. Do you have a lawyer?"

"Not me," said Joe. "Never cared for 'em."

"In that event, you'll be assigned one," said Tuffo. "Is this clear to you, so far?"

"Sure," said Joe. "Whaddaya think I am, senile or somethin'?"

"Just want to be sure you're aware of your rights," said Tuffo. He sighed. "You'll be arraigned before a U.S. Commissioner, and I guarantee you that your bail will be set so high you'll be unable to make it." Tuffo sighed again. "Look, none of us, nobody, really wants to see an elderly man like yourself locked up in a cell. I mean, I got a father who's just about your age. The point I'm—"

"Save the speech," said Joe. "I'm guilty, I admit it."

"You're missing—"

"I ain't missing nothing," said Joe, "except maybe a little hair on top."

"Joe, so far, your accomplices haven't been found, nor has the money been recovered. If you were to cooperate with us on these matters—and believe me, we'll locate everything and everyone with or without your assistance—I think that the Bureau could legitimately stress your cooperation when bail is fixed."

Joe pretended to think. "How'd you get us?" he said after a moment. "Fingerprints?"

Tuffo sat on a corner of the table. "All over the place. Someone got a partial on the license plate of that cab you took. We got a statement from the driver. We found the bag you discarded in the subway, got prints off that. We found bills from the robbery on the platform. Joe, believe me, the case is closed."

Joe shrugged. "Next time, I'll know to wear gloves."

"Joe, about the others—"

"They're where you can't get them," said Joe. "They've left, and they're safe."

"Have they fled the country, Joe?" asked Tuffo.

"They've fled the world," said Joe. "And who the hell gave you permission to call me Joe? Show some respect for your elders, will ya?"

● ● ● ●

It was two weeks since Joe's arrest.

Agent Jensen, from the Washington office, walked rapidly down the hallway of the Federal Detention Center. He hated New York, hated the air, the traffic, the garbage. Most particularly, he hated the people. The New York guys were a breed apart; they regarded the Washington headquarters as a nuisance, to be granted lip service only, and then ignored. Even when they'd failed miserably at something, as they had in this case, they still maintained that patronizing air of superiority. As if success in matters of this type wasn't worth *their* efforts.

"You people here still have no grasp of the power of public relations," he said now, his heels clicking on the marble. Alongside him, Tuffo strained to keep up.

"We did everything we could," said Tuffo. "There are limits."

"Sure," said Jensen gruffly. "You did wonderfully. This whole thing is great. I got nothing better to do than fly all the way up here to baby-sit for you guys."

They climbed a flight of stairs. Tuffo was breathing heavily.

"The old son of a bitch has no record," continued Jensen. "Probably never even lifted a bottle of Geritol, and the whole goddamn New York City office can't get dick out of him."

"He's a tough old coot," said Tuffo.

"Really?" said Jensen, his voice choked with contempt. "Well, if he doesn't open up for me, I'm gonna fry the hoary bastard." They passed through the large bullpen area with its randomly scattered desks. "Do you know what's gonna happen if he gets away with this?"

"I believe so," said Tuffo.

"'I believe so,'" mimicked Jensen. "A moron could tell you what. In one week's time, every geezer in the goddamn country who can get his hands on a water pistol, every dried-out, herniated, arthritic old fart who's tired of leaning on his cane, will be out sticking up their local banks and candy stores." He pushed open the door to the interrogation room.

233

Three agents sat at the table, drinking coffee from styrofoam cups. At the far end of the room, Joe was picking his nose. Over the past two weeks he'd gotten to know this room very well, gotten to know each of the agents well too. He had told the young lawyer from Legal Aid not to bother showing up today, pledged that he would say nothing. "What can they do to me?" he argued, and the attorney had reluctantly agreed.

Joe looked up as Jensen came toward him.

"Hello, Mr. Harris, I'm Bob Jensen from the Washington office."

"Hi," said Joe. "How are you?"

"Mr. Harris, I'll get right to the point. I've been asked to come down here because our people in the capital thought they heard that you might be a little reluctant to cooperate with our men in the local office. Actually, it's not that unusual a situation. Personally speaking, from what I can tell about the case—"

"Excuse me, Sonny Boy, one second," said Joe.

"Mr. Harris, if you'll—"

"Maybe I can save you some of your valuable time. I mean, from the capital yet . . . I'm flattered, but like I already told your buddies here—I'm guilty. Me and my two friends robbed the bank."

"Mr. Harris, we know that. The problem—"

"The problem is we did it, and we buried the money, and I ain't ever gonna tell you where. And you sure as hell ain't never gonna find it on your own. So why don't you just lock me up and forget about this whole thing. You'll be doing everyone a favor."

Jensen sat down on a chair. He smiled patiently. "They tell me, Joe, that you don't have any record at all. In fact, there is every indication that you've been a law-abiding and productive member of your community since . . . well, let's face it . . . since a long time before I learned how to walk."

The blond agent, who was chewing gum, chuckled affably. Even Tuffo forced a smile.

"Joe," Jensen continued, "your history, along with the fact that this whole incident has become a widely publicized social issue, has helped a lot of forces, including ourselves, to rally to your support. Bet you didn't know you had fans right here in the Bureau, did you, Joe?"

"Could've fooled me, Sonny Boy."

"But look," said Jensen, suddenly serious, "you're gonna have to meet us half way on this. Now, I can't promise you, but if you show us that you've changed your attitude, I think there's an excellent chance you'll be able to walk away from this whole mess."

"You mean, you'll just let me go?"

"I mean"—Jensen leaned forward to emphasize the words—"*scot-free.*" Sincerity oozed from all his pores.

Joe cocked his head thoughtfully, inhaled, then glanced toward the agent who was chewing gum. "Got an extra piece?"

The agent looked at Jensen, received a nod, then handed over a stick of gum.

"Thanks," said Joe. "I should really stick to the sugarless, but what the hell, I figure this here is a special occasion." Slowly, he unwrapped the gum and put it in his mouth.

"So, whaddaya say, Joe?" asked Jensen.

The room was absolutely still.

Joe looked up, his jaws working. His eyes met

235

Jensen's. "I say, why don't you get the fuck outta here, Sonny Boy. You give me a headache." He turned to the blond agent. "You wouldn't have another piece, would you?"

● ● ● ●

A few days later, Pete stood before a desk marked *Visitors*. The only other furnishings in the long green room were two rows of straight chairs separated by a comb of plexiglass partitions.

"Can I help you?" asked the uniformed officer at the desk.

"Yeah . . . uh . . . a friend of mine is in here, and I was told I could come and visit him."

"Inmate's name?"

"Joe Harris."

The officer made notes on a form. "Your name?"

"Peter McCaffrey."

"You have identification, Mr. McCaffrey?"

Pete produced his driver's license. The officer copied down the number, then motioned to another guard, who took the form and left the room. "Go down to station number sixteen and have a seat," the desk man told Pete. "He'll be out in a minute."

"Thanks," said Pete. He made his way along the thick plexiglass. About half the stations were empty; the rest were occupied by urgently conversing people. Though Pete could not hear any of the words, the quality of all the exchanges seemed the same— desperate, anxious, pleading. He found Station 16 and sat down. A fluorescent light above him blinked disconcertingly; its transformer hummed. Plaster was peeling from the walls. The vinyl asbestos tiles underfoot were beginning to loosen and curl. A place full of rot and decay, thought Pete. Not a place for an old man. The rusted metal door on the opposite side of the partition swung open, and Joe came stiffly forward. He smiled as he plopped into the chair.

"Hiya, Pete."

"Hi, Joe."

"They're gonna make me go to lunch in about a minute, so we're gonna have to keep this kinda short."

Pete nodded. Joe looked tired, a bit thinner perhaps, but not as bad as he'd feared. "Kathy sends her love. She wanted to come down and see you, too, but we couldn't get anyone to watch the kids."

"That's okay," said Joe. "Don't you worry none. You give her my best, hear?"

"Sure," said Pete.

Joe looked off to the side. "You know my only regret in all of this? I missed Al's funeral. Everything else is hunky-dory, but that. . . ." He sighed. "Well, I just would've liked to say good-bye, that's all."

"It was a good funeral, Joe. He had a nice casket." Pete paused. "How, uh, do you like that lawyer they gave you?"

"The kid?"

Pete smiled. "Yeah."

"He's okay. Seems fine."

"I spoke with him."

Joe's eyes widened. His face grew anxious. "What do you mean? About what?"

Pete lifted his palm. "Don't worry, I didn't tell him nothing. We just talked a little about the case. He says they're gonna be a lot tougher on you than you thought, if you don't give them back the money."

Joe stiffened. "Yeah? Well, screw them."

"I dunno, Joe. Maybe you should just return the money from the robbery."

Joe shook his head. "Forget it. Al and Willie would drop dead twice if I did that. No, sir." He hesitated. "Besides, Pete . . . let me tell you something. For the last couple years, me, Al, and Willie all sat on that park bench and looked at each other. Maybe a politician would come around and talk to us at election time, but that was about it. That was our life. Here, I got my own cell with a toilet and a sink. The food's okay, and I'm feeling good. As a matter of fact, they treat me like a king around here. Everyone comes around to talk, and they all wanna do me favors." Joe's eyes twinkled. "And it'll be the same anywhere they send me. I guarantee it. Because sooner or later, after a while, after they think I'm softened up, they'll all come around asking me where I hid the money. They don't know it, but every one of 'em is older than me, and besides—"

The metal door opened, and a guard came in. "All right, we're gonna have to wrap it up now."

Joe shrugged and gave Pete a long, direct look. "Inside or out," he said, "I'm a prisoner either way. So don't worry about me, Pete. You just enjoy all your inheritance, and take real good care of Kathy and the kids. Al would've wanted that."

Pete chewed his lip. "Joe—"

"Okay, let's get going," interrupted the guard.

Joe rose and moved toward the door. When h was halfway through it, however, he spun around an yelled, "Besides . . . no tin-horn joint like this could ever hold me!"

The last thing Pete saw, before the metal door swung shut, was Joe's elfish grin.

# BEST-SELLING MOVIE HITS
# FROM WARNER BOOKS

## ALIEN
*by Alan Dean Foster*                      (82-977, $2.25)

The seven space travelers had left their own universe behind, and now their monitor told them that on the planet revolving below them, someone was signaling for help. By space law, they must descend, explore and render assistance. Who could tell what being called to them —or why? All they knew was that it was Alien. THE NATIONAL BESTSELLER BASED ON THE SMASH HIT MOVIE!

## THE ROSE                          *Available in November*
*by Leonore Fleischer*                    (82-996, $2.25)

Somewhere there's perfection, but a woman can lose everything by trying to sing one perfect song, to find one perfect love, to be one perfect rose. THE ROSE—No drug, no drink, no ecstatic round of applause, not even the understanding of a man who can glimpse her inner pain can stop her from ruining everything by trying to get what she wants from herself. Soon-to-be-released film from 20th Century-Fox starring Bette Midler.

## BREAKING AWAY
*by Joseph Howard*                        (90-172, $1.95)

The college kids called them "Cutters." They were the guys who didn't go to college in a college town—outsiders in the place where they were born! Maybe that's why Mike, who had been a high school quarterback, was a menace on wheels when he drove his car down Fraternity Row. But now the Cutters had a chance to compete in the Little 500 Bike Race. They could prove they really counted—especially to themselves!

## HARDCORE
*by Leonard Schrader*                     (89-657, $1.95)

Kristen was lovely, innocent, just fifteen—off on a church outing. And now she's gone! Terrified that he'll find her too late, her father, Jake Zondervan, makes a pilgrimage into the hellish pit of West Coast porn culture to search for a nameless girl in a dirty movie—a girl who was once his daughter.